HERE WITH THE SHADOWS

Here with the Shadows

by

Steve Rasnic Tem

Swan River Press
Dublin, Ireland
MMXXIV

Here with the Shadows
by Steve Rasnic Tem

Published by
Swan River Press
at Æon House
Dublin, Ireland
June MMXXIV

www.swanriverpress.ie
brian@swanriverpress.ie

Cover design by Meggan Kehrli
from "Smuggling the Dead" (2013)
by Jason Zerrillo

Set in Garamond by Ken Mackenzie

Paperback Edition
ISBN 978-1-78380-773-4

Swan River Press published
a limited hardback edition of
Here with the Shadows in February 2014.

Contents

Here with the Shadows

Jewel was surprised to find her dad waiting for her on the sidewalk, his last bundle of mementoes wrapped like a child in his arms. She wasn't late. He could be impulsive; she tried never to be late where he was concerned.

She got out of the car and hurried up the steps. "Dad? Is something wrong? Why are you waiting out here?"

He blinked at her a few times before speaking, his eyes wet and shiny. He did that a lot these days. Not as if he didn't remember her. More as if he remembered too much.

"I got finished with my goodbyes early, I guess. I didn't want to wait in an empty house."

"Okay . . . but I'd like my last look."

"Sure, go ahead. I'll wait out here."

"Dad, at least sit down."

"Okay." He put the bundle on the ground and plopped down on the step so fast it made her gasp. "I'll just wait here." When she was a kid she'd thought that when he sounded like this it meant he was mad at her. Maybe there was some anger, but she'd learned it wasn't about her.

"Dad."

"Go on, I'll be okay. I won't wander off. Promise."

"I'll just be a minute."

If anything made it clear it wasn't her home anymore it was seeing it empty. Greyish rectangular patches in the polished wood told her where the furniture used to be, but at the moment she couldn't remember which piece went where. Her steps echoed too loudly, like something invisible beating on the door. Window panes rattled as if tapped. She'd done that once when she was eight. Dad had sat with her for two hours while she cried for her cut finger, and for Mom.

She hadn't lived in this house for about ten years, but she'd visited him almost every week. It was still home, until today. She kept glancing out the front windows. Dad still sat there, as he'd promised. Alec said her Dad should stay with them. "Alec's a good man," Dad had replied. "You don't let this one go, you hear?" She'd blanched at that, feeling criticised. "But I don't want you watching me grow old every day." And that was that.

Outside she made herself beam. "So you ready for your new life?" She said it a little too loudly, a little too eagerly. He laughed, obviously seeing right through her, but he didn't say anything. This was the man who'd told her "when one door closes, another always opens", practically every other day of her life. She'd listened to it eagerly when she was little, as if it held a magic secret; resentfully when she was a teenager, thinking it the corniest thing she'd ever heard; and now she still thought it corny, but occasionally found herself giving out the same advice.

The drive from the old house to that Sixties development in the suburbs was a good hour, but only ten minutes via interstate from her own place, so checking in on Dad would be easy. He sat quietly in the passenger seat while she tried to think of what to say. Sometimes trying to make him feel better about something only seemed to agitate him more, as if he just wanted her to shut up.

After awhile he looked back. It made her sad. Then a few minutes later he repeated the motion. Then again a few minutes after that. She watched him more closely this time—he wasn't looking through the back window; he was glancing into the back seat.

"Dad? Something back there?"

"No, I—" He laughed softly. "I just had a strange notion. For some reason I expected to see someone sitting there. Now, I hasten to add, I did not see anyone sitting there. I'm not crazy you know. But for some reason I expected it. It's like sometimes you don't expect to see someone in a place, but then there they are. But sometimes, I think, there's this empty place, there's no one there, but for some reason you expect someone to be there. And because they're not there, you miss them. I'm not making any sense, am I?"

She didn't know what to say. "I was never good with philosophy, you know."

"You're good at living your life. I think that's all you need. Do you remember your first day of third grade? Your mom and I, we decided you'd take the school bus that year, so I drove you to the stop. I wasn't so sure. Hell, I almost went on the school bus with you. I would've sat in the class room with you if they'd let me. But your mom said this would be good for you, and she was usually right about those things.

"I remember standing there and holding your hand, waiting. You trembled so. And if I hadn't been scared of what your mother would say, I would have left my car parked there, and I would've gotten on that bus."

Jewel smiled, even though she'd heard this story a hundred times before. "That was almost a year before she died, wasn't it? By the time I started fourth grade she was gone."

"Yep."

"She was right, you know—it was good that I learned early on how to ride the bus."

"She was always right." She saw him start to look into the back seat again, but he stopped himself.

"Dad, did you not remarry because you had me to take care of? Because you could have, you know?"

He was quiet for awhile, fidgeting. He looked out the passenger window a few times. She almost thought he'd forgotten the question when he said, "Don't blame yourself for that. I certainly could have. I'm not even sure why I didn't.

"It's just that there's this world full of people, people everywhere you look, leading their complicated lives, because every life is more complicated than it looks. And then there is this world of those who have passed, not ghosts exactly, but their remembered presence, and those memories, well, they're everywhere, and if you multiply that by this factor that we all see things differently, that people may remember a person a hundred different ways in a hundred different places, then it's just staggering, isn't it? The sheer numbers, the spaces occupied both in your surroundings and in your head.

"Some afternoons I swear you can hear people thrumming, the vibrations of their lives, the emotion left by their passage, shaking the ground, filling the air with waves of sound and movement.

"The first few years after your mother died I was so shaken, so filled with grief that I stepped away from all that. I just, stepped away. I had no idea how to raise a child without her, so I read and I studied and I asked so many questions of the other parents in your school, in the neighbourhood, anyone I ran into, really. And once I learned enough, well, I found I liked the simplicity of it, the clarity. You needed certain things—clothes, food, education, entertainment—I applied myself to that, and it was fulfilling. It made sense to me. Nothing else did.

"Sometimes I imagined myself dating a woman. I imagined myself being married again. I could see all that in my head. I thought a new mother would even be good for you. But it would mean blending my life into someone else's again. My life with you worked. But this would mean going somewhere where I wasn't sure anything would work. It would mean entering into all that complication again, all that busyness, that noise and vibration, all those presences, all those absences that fill the world, simply a matter of a step in a new direction, and I found I just couldn't do it. I couldn't, sweetheart."

She didn't know what to say. Maybe he was ill, maybe something had gone wrong with him. But she didn't think so. And so she just said, "I know, Dad. I know." Even though she didn't. She just said that and drove.

Her dad's new house was in a quiet neighbourhood of winding streets a few blocks from a major shopping mall. He would have hated that in the old days but now he said he looked forward to the convenience. The ranch style was also not to his usual taste, but they'd hoped it would be kinder to his arthritis and he said it seemed easy and comfortable. This wasn't anything like the house she grew up in, but she would have loved it here as a little girl.

He'd hired some ladies to help him arrange the furniture, but this would be his first night sleeping here. And this would be the first time Jewel had been here with it completely furnished.

He led her in slowly. He was so cute, he seemed so proud. But she couldn't say that. "It looks wonderful," she said from the entrance, and he guided her through the floor plan telling her what room in the old house each piece had come from, which of course she already knew, and why he had chosen the new placement, which mostly she could not follow.

"I put the sideboard here because this space reminds me of both a dining room and a living room even though I plan to use this for neither. When the new bookshelves come they'll go in here and the sideboard will be used to store mail, which seems logical when you think about it."

She said, "That's great, Dad." The walls of one bedroom were covered with probably every photograph ever taken of her, arranged in great swirls and flowing patterns that must have taken those women hours to do while her dad directed them. The display embarrassed her terribly, but still moved her to tears.

He was focused enough as he conducted the tour, but now and again he would stop and stare a little too long at something, sometimes lowering his glasses to do so. Shadowed corners seemed to distract him, so every time he noticed one he apparently had to stop and get his bearings again, as if the angles at which the walls came together to make these corners bothered him, or as if something were standing there inside the corner that made no sense.

Sometimes when they passed through a doorway he would back out again, glance left or right, and go back through to the other side, and likewise look left or right, as if comparing things on both sides of the wall. The most unsettling thing was that he wouldn't say what he was doing or why, just introduce his odd interludes with an "excuse me", and ending them with, "sorry, let's go on".

They were in the back yard now and the sunset was beautiful, and so many of the plants beginning to bloom. "The real estate agent told me the former owners were gardeners," she said. "Out here there are forty different flowering plants. Can you imagine?"

But Dad was looking back at the house, shading his eyes with his hand as if trying to make something out. "I think there are lights out here, for at night? I believe you told me there are lights out here," he said.

"The switch is by the door. You look so tired. Should I go so you can rest, or should I stay awhile?"

He turned and smiled at her. "It's a really lovely place."

"Yes, it is, Dad."

"I'm going to be happy here, I think. It's just so great. You know, it's like living in the afterlife."

He didn't sleep much that first night. It wasn't as if there were noises that disturbed him. There were hardly any noises at all. But it was like in the car that day. It seemed he was expecting something, someone. And when whatever it was failed to arrive he didn't quite know what to make of it. He woke up tired and gritty-eyed and too anxious to stay in bed.

Before buying the house he'd rarely been in this part of the city. Except before, when he was a child. This had been mostly farms down here when he was just a young boy, with great stretches of sparse development in between. His grandfather had had a small farm with a vegetable garden and some chickens. He'd spent several summers chasing the chickens and running over the small hills swollen with tall grasses. Sometimes he'd find old wagon parts in the grass, or a curved piece of barrel. Sometimes he'd find arrowheads in the freshly ploughed fields.

It was a warm morning so he decided to go for a walk. His legs had been better, but he brought his cane anyway in case they started feeling like two broken sticks. He was pleased when several neighbours waved to him, and when one commented that she'd seen him move in. Someone driving by, he supposed a neighbour, stuck his head out the window and asked him if he'd like a ride to wherever he was going. He supposed the fellow had seen his cane, noticed his age. He told him no thanks. He didn't want people looking at him like he was some old man needing a ride.

He crossed several streets then headed up the long curving road that bordered the large oval of concrete and asphalt of the shopping mall. He could see a movie theatre, several restaurants, and a book store he'd have to check out. It wasn't the old neighbourhood, but he could certainly make it do.

What he wanted was to find where his grandfather's house had been. He knew the old road had turned into an east/west highway where the mall lay now, and his grandfather's place had been on a rise just beyond that. The view had been remarkable—you could see clear through to the foothills of the Rockies simply by turning your head west. From his granddad's front door you could see the distant, and then much smaller, downtown. "Million dollar view," Granddad had called it, with no exaggeration. The boy he'd been, whose life he remembered as being close and heated and small, had felt like the crown prince when he'd stayed there, surveying his kingdom.

The day he found the stone pile out behind his granddad's house had been one of those bright days, a warm breeze coming off the fields. He'd been running through the tall grass, pretending it was a giant dry ocean, his eyes almost closed, feeling the stems slap against his open palms until they were almost painful, but not quite. His toe hit the first stone and he almost tumbled into the pile. He stared. The tall grass had been cleared slightly away from this one spot, where there was a pile of rocks both jagged and rounded on the corners. The bottom ones were mostly buried in the ground, and the row above that had ground between the rocks like mortar, and the ones on top were looser and had space in between. And at the very top an old tarnished belt buckle had been jammed between two of them. It was scratched up and stained. He went to get it out.

"I wouldn't climb on them rocks if I was you," his granddad's voice said behind him.

He turned around and had to hide his eyes from the sun. His granddad's head was this dark shape against the sky. His granddad was the tallest man he'd ever seen. "Why not?"

"I seen snakes in that pile last summer."

He went to his granddad's side, terrified. "Are those from an old building?"

"No, I reckon it's a grave. Pioneer most likely. Or it could'a been an Indian—I don't know what their customs were back then. Whoever it was must've died out here, and friends buried the poor soul, using that buckle to at least give it a little show, then they must've moved on."

He'd stared at it a different way then, like it marked the loneliest spot on the earth. "How long has it been here?"

"No idea—it was here when I built this house."

"Did you tell anybody?"

"No, and I'd be obliged if you didn't, either. A grave like that should be left alone, and people now, well, they could be more respectful than they are."

He stared at it a long time, afraid he might start crying, until his granddad laid a hand on his shoulder. "It's okay to be soft about it, Jim. Don't let nobody tell you different. I know you always take things hard. And that's a hard row to hoe."

He saw the grave on a few visits after that, but mostly he just avoided it. And by the time he was a teenager he forgot about it for a few years.

Finding the spot where granddad's farm had been proved impossible. The ground had been rearranged, sculpted, no doubt a half-dozen times since then. There was no rising hill anymore. It levelled out, and then there was a wide, shallow valley behind the mall that hadn't been there before, full of trees and houses. That old road that used to lead out to this part of the country had just been scraped out and paved, and a ditch dug out alongside it. The easiest thing for the highway builders would have been just to follow the terrain. He remembered how it seemed they'd had to go up and down over every little hill to get here. Now, well, they had giant machines that could move tons at a time, and make practically any landscape you wanted. No doubt the pieces of granddad's farm were now scattered all over. And that grave. Not just here, but the whole world was a rearrangement.

But here and there were what looked to be old strips of prairie: between two sidewalks, along a road, behind that fence, and between this sidewalk and the mall. Slices and peels of it. The grass wasn't as tall as he remembered, but it looked related, and it bent the same way in the wind.

He found one of those strips, and he eased himself down to the ground. Jewel would have told him he was making himself sick—what if he couldn't get up again? —but Jewel wasn't here.

From this vantage the ground appeared uneven, the prairie sections the worst, but the other grassy parts as well, even the stretches of concrete and asphalt. You wouldn't necessarily see them when standing up, and even if you saw one, some cool spot making the simmering heat around it appear even hotter, it might not register. People had grown accustomed to shadow and mirage.

He'd thought about that grave for days, wondering how many more there were in the world like that, marked and unmarked, places where you tucked away a loved one and then moved on. How many people had come and gone from the world and lay stretched out or curled up in the ground. How many folk you talked about a little bit less every day until even their names, unimportant to history, were gone? He could not bear the math of it, could not sort the figures out in his head, and so he'd gotten little sleep and walked about dazed that last week of summer, and his granddad had sent him home, thinking him ill.

He'd wanted to tell his granddad what was really bothering him but just couldn't bring himself to say out loud the words. Even now, an old man, he wasn't sure he really understood the nature of it. How many lives, how many bodies, how many memories, how much grief could one world hold? Was it possible they'd one day fill it up and be forced to leave rather than live in a graveyard?

He'd never talked to his daughter about it, because he would have imagined her particular death, and he could not do that.

Something was standing a few yards back on his left. He hadn't noticed it before, and now noticed only its shadow. At first he thought it was a tree, even though there were no trees in the vicinity, just a few narrow saplings. He turned his head slowly in that direction.

There appeared to be a vertical tear in reality, a flaw in the fabric of the atmosphere, although he doubted such flaws were possible. It was so like a tear, with something peeking through from the other side, and the flaps created by the tear turning inside out and showing. It appeared to be a woman, or her shadow, because it was grey, and of reduced opacity.

Maybe his retina was tearing, as much as he read, as much as he simply looked at things, so intently, afraid to miss anything. He'd seen things, or anticipated seeing things, for weeks now. He'd had that sensation on his final visit to the old house—that was why he had waited outside for Jewel.

Then there in the back seat of the car and in the new house as well, as if memory had reached its maximal limits, and were bursting through into immediacy.

He looked away from the grey figure standing so still there, so like a statue, but saw that it was happening all over the hillside, and down into the shallow asphalt and concrete saucer of the mall: these vertical tears, and the shadowed statues slipping through, motionless and quiet as they stared out at what the world had become.

He struggled to his feet, afraid he might not make it, his arm and the cane shaking with his effort. He headed down the sidewalk as quickly as possible toward his new home, that warm and comfortable place where things were apt to be better and he could listen to music and read.

But he kept saying "excuse me", because he'd been raised that way. When bumping into people you said excuse me, even if they were statues or shadows or dead. Because they filled the sidewalk now, so thickly like a forest jammed with dead and unharvested trees, and he could not move without bumping into one. They were suddenly everywhere, at last beginning to move, milling about as if they had no idea where they were going or even what they were, just so many shadows filling the sidewalks and the world and obscuring whatever colour might have been left for him.

They were waiting at the house, so many of them, but he had things to do, dinner to make and then the music and the reading, all the things he'd planned out for his remaining years. And so he lived with them as best he could, saying "excuse me" a bit less as time wore on, because manners were exhausting when so frequently applied. But some days they left almost no room for him. And some days with their numbers he could hardly breathe.

Jewel spent a couple of weeks closing up her father's house. She could have done it more quickly, but she wanted to take her time going through things, remembering what he'd valued and loved, and trying to find some suitable home for it all. She had bookish friends who appreciated his library, and there were charities for the clothes and some of the other things. She would take very little for herself both because they hadn't much room and because her father wouldn't have wanted her to take on more than she could handle.

Alec was a great help, leaving her alone when she needed it, and hauling box after box to where they needed to go. He wanted a couple of the nicer books for himself because they reminded him of her father.

There had been no deterioration his last year, unless he'd hidden it from her. But there had been an increase in his distraction, a more intense version of what she'd seen that day in the car and at the new house. Now and then he'd say "excuse me", as if apologising to her for it. She'd kept assuring him it was okay, and there was no need to apologise. But then he'd look at her with this puzzled expression, and the apologies would continue, usually softly, or under his breath, like a constant mantra he used to relax himself.

The final day she stood in the empty house saying goodbye to the last of it, her eyes full of tears. Things blurred and melted and ran down her face, and now and then the house felt crowded, as if she hadn't moved anything at all. As if the world had suddenly grown so full it would soon push her out.

Before she left she stood gazing out at the back yard, the late afternoon sun making the back fence suddenly golden, and when she blinked the yard was full of greyish statues, like the back lot of one of those monument companies, and when she blinked again they were gone, and she was thinking she must be her father's daughter when she saw him, standing with his back to her, so quiet as he took it all in, the fullness and the absolute impossibility, the world.

A House by the Ocean

She had to park the rental car out on the main road and walk the rest of the way, taking just a few clothes and a present for her niece in the backpack that had been her carry-on. If things went well enough with her sister—and there was just no predicting—maybe she could come back for the rest of her luggage. Maybe they had a pickup or something that would run on that debris- and sand-laden lane the sign promised was Ocean Way. Or maybe not. Her sister Karen had always been dismissive of things other people thought practical, or even essential.

Lauren's annoyance gathered as she stepped carefully through the tangle of branches and fallen leaves under the canopy of tree limbs, the sounds of her progress disappearing into the unstable soil that covered the invisible road. But she was twenty years out of practice being angry with her sister—she couldn't maintain it, even in the aftermath of all those years thinking Karen was dead. As the wind picked up and rattled the limbs above, the fragmented shadows swarming like the spirits of a thousand broken birds, she began to cry as both regret and anxiety fought to consume her.

She made her way out to where the trees stopped altogether and the ground dropped swiftly into the oceanfront. The demarcation was so defined she wondered if the shoreline might have changed because of some calamity, or the ocean had receded after having taken its last bite. She'd never spent much time near the ocean, and was sure this visit wouldn't change that. How did her sister live with that constant rumbling wall?

For a few minutes she simply stared at the heaving, changing waters. The view held neither the sameness nor the peacefulness she might have expected. There was such a lack of defining form, such terrible possibility—how had those early sailors crossed its landless expanses without their minds dissolving in the terror of its scale?

Even perched a couple of hundred yards from its edge, she felt at risk to body and soul. She was an educated person, but what she saw made no sense to her, inspired silliness and superstition: the ocean appeared so high, what held it back? Suddenly it had made her a child again.

Her eyes had been on the house for several moments before she realised what she was seeing. It stood among those huge rocks not too far from the beach, and had that same sort of blockiness and a similar colouring of dark grey going to black in spots. It leaned a bit, or seemed to, away from the ocean, and she couldn't tell if some of the odd angles above the windows and just under the roof were purposeful examples of eccentric craft or simply evidence of structural damage. It looked abandoned—no curtains she could see, or anything outside indicating a family lived there, and there were great bands of crystalline silt deposited near the bottom, as if those parts upon occasion had been submerged.

Lauren had called her once, after Hurricane Fran landed on the North Carolina coast in 1996. She used to have a torn piece of paper on the refrigerator with the phone number scribbled on it. "Why wouldn't I be okay?" Karen had snapped, as if it had been an offensive question. "I can take care of myself!" And then she'd hung up. It was the same old argument they'd been having ever since their mother died. But Lauren was the older one—of course she felt some added responsibility. If she came off too strong sometimes it was only because she cared.

She'd called that number again in 1999 after Floyd hit. It had been disconnected. She wrote a letter but it was returned. She'd contacted mutual friends. No one had heard from Karen since the hurricane. She thought about flying out there then, but she had her job, and Karen would have just dumped all kinds of abuse on her for her troubles. So finally she'd let it go. She'd done her share. Let Karen contact her if she wanted to stay in touch.

The lane began to fade halfway along the slope and eventually disappeared among the scattered clumps of salt grass. There were no signs of ruts, so she assumed Karen must not own a vehicle. Maybe she shouldn't have come, but Karen had called at last, needing her, sounding nothing like the resentful younger sister from their last conversation. The weight of the ocean air pushed against her face brought her to the verge of tears.

"Sis?" Her sister's voice had sounded thin and reedy, and even further away than North Carolina. There was a hiss on the line, and the occasional watery echo that might have been interference, or a sob, or the surrounding ocean, rising.

"Karen? Honey, it's been a long time."

There was just a moment's hesitation, and in that moment Lauren thought she heard a child crying. "Sis . . . we need you to come out here," Karen sounded stressed out of her mind. Another pause, and in that a child's intemperate scream. A girl, maybe. Lauren had never had kids, but for a child to make a sound like that, it unsettled her.

"Karen, is there a child there?"

"Julieee . . . " The name trailed out, in sadness, or because her sister was trying to calm the child, Lauren couldn't tell.

"I didn't know. Is she yours?"

"Seven years. Please come, soon as you can . . . " Karen's voice had a hollow sound.

"Is it the same place? Did you move?"

"Same . . . always been here . . . " Her sister's voice was lost to the echo and static hiss.

She'd tried several times to call her back with no luck. The line sounded weak or distorted, or there was no sound at all, not even a ring. The next day she purchased her plane ticket. She bought Julie a doll on her way to the airport, a floppy thing with huge, aimless eyes.

Lauren found the entrance to the house, a single narrow door that faced the ocean, but it had been placed about a third of the way up the structure, on a porch apparently accessible only by means of several sets of stairs that were staggered across the rocks and appeared to have been constructed from old water-logged timbers, many with cracked and collapsed surfaces and splintered ends, and decorated with scattered white furry streaks she assumed to be some variety of mould.

The whole assemblage appeared unsafe for a child, or anyone else, for that matter. She was feeling a familiar, nagging outrage over her sister's irresponsibility, before it occurred to her that of course Karen couldn't possibly live here. She must have abandoned this ruin ages ago, and for some reason assumed Lauren had her newer address.

But then something up on the porch caught her eye, some shape near one corner, almost but not quite out of her line of sight. Rough-formed head and maybe a beak, some sort of huge dark sea bird peering down at her. Unmoving, patiently waiting. And that led her eyes to the window above and to the right of it, and the face of the little girl on the other side of the glass looking out.

Lauren went up a few steps carefully. The wood was mushy. Moisture was weeping out around her shoes. She took another few steps and could feel the timbers shifting, barely gripped by the wet and rusted nails. A large flat expanse of rock made a landing before the next flight of steps began at its far end. She walked across the rock feeling more secure; the next steps looked drier, but groaned when her feet came down on them. The rough-hewn stair stringer wiggled, but the rickety frame held. She came to the next landing, which was just a few planks attached to an old beam bolted to another rock. It was too narrow to be safe, she thought, especially for a little girl, and she stepped quickly on to it and off again, and after a few more nervous steps—she seemed so high now—she was standing on one end of the porch.

The ugly sea bird stared at her, its neck bent awkwardly. It was just a strange and heavy twist of driftwood, she now saw, which someone had apparently treasured enough to risk a dangerous haul up here for display.

She walked slowly over to the window. The girl's face looked up at her, then vanished into the grubby darkness of the room, but not before Lauren had been struck by the remarkable family resemblance to Karen, to their mother, and to Lauren herself.

She went to the heavily-weathered door and knocked, waited, and knocked again. She tried the greenish knob and after the momentary resistance of swollen wood the door popped open.

It took a while for her eyes to adjust, and when they did she was disappointed by the dust-furred interior, the ridges of grime on the floor, the dirty bottles and corroded pans, the water stains on the walls as large and complex as duotone landscapes, the stench of mould.

Her tears welled up—she hadn't realised just how much she'd hoped—when the ocean hissed behind her as the dying waves raced over the pebbled shore, and Karen drifted in and wrapped her arms around her, whispering "Sis", and folding her seemingly weightless body into Lauren's embrace.

They held each other and cried, and over Karen's shoulder Lauren watched as that lovely little girl came in and smiled, holding up a lantern, and in that warmer light she could see how mistaken she had been. The room was poor but clean, and invited her with its array of quilts and pillows and cushioned chairs, handcrafts hanging on the walls, and everywhere she looked an array of colours and intriguing shapes. The decay and disorder had been a product of the shadows, she thought, and the angle of the light, aided by her distress and fatigue.

The two sisters talked long into the night, Julie asleep across a blanket at her mother's feet. She held the doll Lauren had given her lightly in her hand.

"I was afraid to tell you," Karen said again. "I've messed up so many times." She sat with her knees up, narrow arms binding herself to herself. Her face was worn, and wearied with stress lines across her forehead, slashing over her cheeks so deeply they looked like scars in the spongy, unhealthily pale skin. Lauren couldn't ever remember her sister being so frighteningly skinny. And yet it oddly made her look younger than she was, like an undernourished teenager. She was also rocking, so subtly that at first Lauren hadn't noticed it. Then she realised it closely matched the rhythm of the waves breaking outside. In fact the whole house appeared to have a sway to it, but that had to be the wind, not the waves.

"We all make mistakes, hon," she told her, reaching out her hand, but for some reason reluctant to touch that fragile body wound so tightly. "If you'd been around you'd have witnessed far too many of mine."

Karen nodded ever so slightly, but didn't look at her. In fact Lauren had noticed her sister's eyes had so far completely avoided any direct contact. The poor kid seemed so ashamed, so distracted, her mind hardly there in the room. Was she at least partly responsible? She'd been the one to raise Karen those last few years of high school.

"I had a husband, Paul. He drowned when Hurricane Fran came ashore. I know I was harsh with you on the phone that time—you'd just wanted to see how I was—but I'd never even told you I was married, so how was I going to tell you my husband was dead?"

"We were pretty distant then, as much my fault as yours. But, honey, that doesn't matter now. 'Water under the bridge', like mom always said."

"You always told me I made bad choices. It was true. I had no business being with him. Neither one of us knew what we were doing here. Paul was full of ideas, but he didn't know how to do anything."

"Look at me, Karen. Please, look at me." After a few moments her sister glided her head around, pointing her face at her. But Lauren could still tell she wasn't actually looking at her. Karen's eyes appeared as pale and unfocused as smoke. Maybe that was the best her sister could do for now. She was obviously, seriously, damaged. "It's not your fault. You've done the best you could. I'm sure." Of course Lauren had no idea if Karen had done her best—in fact, that possibility seemed quite remote, but what did the truth of it matter now?

"I've been so lonely since then," Karen said to the window, and the ocean moving so invisibly, and largely, out there. "I've had nothing to do."

Julie stirred then, turning her head to the ceiling. Her face was so white and perfect—like a mask floating up from the depths of her head to the surface and then settling back down again. Lauren yawned. She was exhausted. She'd have to go to bed soon.

"Well, obviously you met someone later, right? And then you had this angel to take care of. That's not exactly nothing."

Karen had closed her eyes. "Nothing," she repeated.

"Before we both fall asleep, is there a spare bedroom? I mean, whatever it is it'll be fine. Or I could sleep right here."

Karen got up without speaking and helped Lauren up a steep and narrow flight of stairs, leaning against her as they ascended, snuggling like a sleepwalker. There were pictures on the walls of people Lauren did not know. Finally they reached a snug little room at the top, a low sprawl of a bed, a skinny window with an eavesdropper's view of the dark waters, the occasional long lines of serrated white illuminated by a full moon. Lauren fell into the covers without undressing, aware of only a whispered goodnight, the cold breath across her face, then oblivion.

She dreamed she fell into the ocean, and even though she couldn't swim all that well the dream didn't bother her, and when she woke up there was no anxiety, only the feeling of a long and tiring trip completed, with Karen waiting at the end.

But somehow she must have fallen out of bed, because now she lay in a sprawl of dirty rags. She looked around—the sun blazed through the narrow curtainless window. And clearly there was no furniture in the room—just these piles of filthy rags, and a few crumbling boxes of warped, waterlogged books, and chewed bits of debris all over the floor, as if rats had been up here doing all the things rats do. She must have wandered away from the guest room upstairs into another, similar room—maybe on the other end—a room that was no longer being used, but then Karen really should have locked it, because Lauren didn't like the idea of Julie wandering in, playing in here.

She went over to the decaying boxes and spent a few minutes looking at the books. They smelled like earth, like the bare moist ground under a big rock you've just pulled up, the exposed worms crawling all around. There were several ancient hardcover novels by authors she had never heard of, an early Southern history, a slim volume concerned with cooking okra, a study of barns of the Carolinas, and a collection of letters between an early governor of North Carolina and his children. If the books had been in better shape, and if she were to stay here for a while, she might have tried to read them. Maybe she still would.

She pushed her face against the window and looked out at the ocean. It was a dark bluish grey today, the sky a stirred expanse of cream above it, heavy with clouds. Visibility was poor. She thought she saw the shape of a distant ship, but it could have been a bird, or driftwood, or anything. She knew, of course, that the rest of the world still carried on while her sister and her niece kept themselves locked away in this isolated house on the coastline. But none of that felt very real while she was here. Time seemed to have given up, because there was nothing to count off, nothing to look forward to. From this angle she felt quite high up in the air; she could feel everything swaying. And yet the ocean was still higher, seeking to invade the sky, and only a trick of physics kept it from invading the land. It all seemed impossible.

She felt vaguely ill, watching the mass of it churning. It was like gazing at a nearby mountain suddenly gone liquid. The roiling waves revealed dark pockets which appeared to have something in them, creatures or spirits or passage to somewhere else, but the pockets collapsed too quickly to tell. She supposed it was akin to seeing shapes in shadow or cloud, but she still could not stop herself from staring and wondering.

As she leaned against the glass she was surprised to feel it give. An arm and a hinge mechanism had been designed to open the window, but the handle was missing so there was no way to pull it shut tightly or latch it firmly. The window was partly open, so she pushed it open some more to lean out for a better look. Maybe she shouldn't have done it, but surely Karen would know how to fix it closed.

She had a good view of the coastline this way, a mile or so north and south. All along the shore the land was dissolving into the aggressive edge of that great body of tortured grey liquid. She had no idea if this meant a storm was coming or if this was the way it looked every day.

She dropped her gaze and saw a large pale bird making its way precariously along the slick rock surfaces between this house and the precipitous edge. Occasionally it would lose its balance and land on its side, then struggle up with hands and feet. Lauren gasped. It was Julie.

"Julieeee . . . " The sounds of her niece's name floated, stretched out and thinned atop a rising gust of wind. Lauren searched frantically for her sister, and then saw Karen struggling up the rocks on the southern edge of the formation, her pale dress soaked and clinging like tissue to her skinny frame. Then Karen was racing across the black and grey stone, but Lauren couldn't see how she could possibly get there in time. So Lauren began shouting, "Julie! Julie!" hoping the child would stop and turn around. The wind reached out and snatched the syllables out of her mouth and flung them at the sky.

The child neared the edge. It was like watching a movie so intently you felt you were actually participating, but then something happened to remind you that most decidedly you were not. Karen's back was blocking Lauren's view of the child. Then a wave hit, drenching them in obscuring spray.

Lauren raced down the stairs, her hands grazing the furry bits of wallpaper and plaster, the cracked walls beginning to come apart and showering the steps in dust and grit. An array of crooked empty picture frames, their surfaces stained green and mould black, shook and tumbled off around her. She had to push her way through a tangle of broken chairs and rotted cardboard at the bottom of the staircase, and manoeuvre around the collapsed table at the centre of the room. Broken fragments of crockery and rusted pans edged a large hole in the warped, stinking floorboards, gaping onto the dark spaces below the abandoned house. Nothing could live in such a place.Nothing could long survive such destruction. Finally she dragged aside the ruins of the half-open front door, the bottom scraping in anguished protest, and stepped gingerly over the trembling porch, careful to avoid the missing and rotted planks.

She found Julie and Karen resting in a shallow place in the rocks. Karen's thin arm lay across the girl's body. Lauren imagined the worst. Then the child's face turned from somewhere within that jumble of wet cloth, pale flesh, and hair, and looked at her, and began to speak, but even getting down on her hands and knees and leaning over as close as possible Lauren could hear no words.

She moved her hands between them, but her fingers would not grab. Their skin was soft, and seemingly edgeless, and moved slowly, or not at all. But eventually they disentangled. Julie sat cross-legged a few feet away, staring out at the ocean. Karen had pulled herself into her sister's arms, and clung there, weeping. Lauren herself was shaking and kept touching Karen's body with her hands to reassure herself, and rubbing her cheek along Karen's face, and kissing her, and softly apologising, but she wasn't sure if Karen could hear, or feel her at all.

"I wish . . . you could take her . . . with you," Karen rasped out. "I never could take . . . the proper care. Is it really too late?"

"Oh, honey, she's yours. She loves you. I can tell."

"No. No," Karen insisted, crying. "It's no good. Please . . . please . . . you can't understand."

Her sister brushed vaguely against her, and she seemed so small, it was like they were kids again, and Lauren wanted so badly to protect her, but didn't know how. It felt as if Karen weighed almost nothing at all. Lauren didn't know if her sister could ever come back from this; there really was no time. She pressed her hands against her, swearing to herself she would never let her go, but it felt as if she already had.

They made their way slowly across the rocks toward the house, Julie in the lead, now moving almost playfully, skipping, with no indication of the danger she'd just been in. Lauren felt unsafe and tried to call the child back, but Karen was so weak, barely there in her torn and disintegrating garment. Lauren couldn't quite get her mouth to make the words. Karen suddenly sighed deeply, and Lauren could smell the stink on her sister's breath, the rotted weed and spoiled fish of it, and the sourness of her hair, like cotton left to soak in rancid water.

She didn't want Julie to reach the house before them, not with all that rotted wood, that grime and rust and breakage, those walls decorated in regret, that life collapsing into ruin. She didn't want to go back in herself, to see again what she'd seen when she came back down the stairs.

"Karen, who is Julie's father? You never said."

The answer came slowly, a whisper wet with emotion. "I don't like . . . I don't think about that."

"It wasn't, well, it couldn't have been Paul, could it? That would be impossible, of course. She's far too young for him to be her dad. Was Paul her father?"

"Yes," her sister sighed, and seemed to fall into nothing, to spread thinly over her, until all Lauren could feel was the damp.

It was then that Julie crossed the rock between Lauren and the sun. In that brief shadow Lauren looked down for her sister, and, not seeing her, turned, and turned again, but Karen was not there, even though Lauren would swear later that she could still smell her on her clothes. Lauren waited for Julie to reappear so that she might hold and reassure her, take the child back with her and make her her own.

She waited the rest of that day and most of the next, then found her way back up the ocean road to her car, and returned home alone.

The Cabinet Child

Around the beginning of the last century, on the outskirts of a small southwest Virginia town which no longer exists, a childless woman named Alma lived with her gentleman farmer husband in a large house up on a ridge. The woman was not childless because of any medical condition—her husband simply felt that children were "ill-advised" in their circumstances, that there was no space for children in the twenty-or-so rooms of what he called their modest home.

Not being of a demonstrative inclination, his wife kept her disappointment largely to herself, but it could not have been more obvious if she had screamed it from their many-gabled roof. Sometimes, in fact, she muttered it in dialogue with whoever should pass, and when no one was looking, she pretended to scream. Over the years despair worked its way into her eyes and drifted down into her cheeks, and the weight of her grief kept her bent and shuffling.

Although her husband Jacob was an insensitive man he was not inobservant. After enduring a number of years of his wife's sad display he apparently decided it gave an inappropriate impression of his household's tenor to the outside world and became determined to do something about it. He did not share his thinking with her directly, of course, but after an equal number of years enduring his maddening obstinacy his wife was well acquainted with his opinions and attitudes. Without so much as a knock he came into her bedroom one afternoon as she sat staring out her window and said, "I have decided you need something to cheer yourself up, my dear. John Hand will be bringing his wagon around soon and you may choose anything on it. Let us call it an early Christmas present, why don't we?"

She looked up at him curiously. After having prayed aloud for some sign of his attention, for so many nights, she could scarcely believe her ears. Was this some trick? As little as it was, still he had never offered her such a prize before. She thought at first that somehow he had hurt his face, and then realised what she had taken for a wound was simply a strained and unaccustomed smile. He carried that awkward smile out the door with him, thank God. She did not think she could bear it if such a thing were running around loose in her private quarters.

John Hand was known throughout the region as a fine furniture craftsman who hauled his pieces around in a large grey wagon as roughly made as his furniture was exquisitely constructed. And yet this wagon had not fallen apart in over twenty years of travels up and down wild hollows and over worn mountain ridges with no paved roads. She had not perused his inventory herself, but people both in town and on the outlying farms claimed he carried goods to suit every taste and had a knack for finding the very thing that would please you, that is, if you had any capacity for being pleased at all, which some folk clearly did not.

Alma had twenty rooms full of furniture, the vast majority of it handed down from various branches of Jacob's family. Alma had never known her husband to be very close to his relations, but any time one of them died and there were goods to be divided he was one of the first to call with his respects. And although he was hardly liked by any of those grieving relatives, he always seemed able to talk them into letting him leave with some item he did not rightly deserve.

Sometimes at night she would catch him with his new acquisitions, stroking and talking to them as if they had replaced the family he no longer much cared for. She could not understand what had come over her that she would have married such a greedy man.

Although she needed no furniture, without question Alma was sorely in need of being pleased, which was why she was at the front gate with an apron pocket full of Jacob's money the next time John Hand came trundling down the road in that horse-drawn wagon full of his wares.

Even though she waved almost frantically Hand did not appear to acknowledge her, but then stopped abruptly in front of their grand gate. She had seen him in town before but never paid him much attention. When Hand suddenly jumped down and stood peering up at her she was somewhat alarmed by the smallness of the man—he was thin as a pin and painfully bent, the top of his head not even reaching to her shoulders, and she was not a particularly tall woman. The wagon loomed like a great ocean liner behind him, and she could not imagine how this crooked little man had filled it with all this furniture, pieces so jammed together it looked like a puzzle successfully completed.

Then Mr. Hand turned his head rather sideways and presented her with a beatific smile, and completely charmed she felt prepared to go with anything the little man cared to suggest.

"A present from the husband, no?"

"Well, yes, he said I could choose anything."

"But not the present madam most wished for." He said it as if it was undeniable fact, and she did not correct him. Surely he had simply guessed, based on some clues in her appearance?

He gazed at her well past the point of discomfort, and then clambered up the side of the wagon, monkey-like and with surprising speed. The next thing she knew he had landed in front of her, holding a small, polished wood cabinet supported by his disproportionately large palm and the cabinet's four unusually long and thin, spiderish legs. "I must confess it has had a previous owner," he said with a mock sad expression. "She was like you, wanting a child so very much. This was to be in the nursery, to hold its dainty little clothes."

Alma was alarmed for a number of reasons, not the least of which that she'd never told the little man that she had wanted a child. Then she quickly realised what a hurtful insult this was on his part—to give someone never to have children a cabinet to hold its clothes? She turned and made for the gate, averting her head so the vicious little man would not see her streaming tears.

"Wait! Please," he said, and a certain softness in his voice stopped her more firmly than a hand on her shoulder ever could. She turned just as he shoved the small cabinet into her open arms. "You will not be—unfulfilled by this gift, I assure you." And with a quick turn he had leapt back onto the seat and the tired-looking horses were pulling him away. She stood awkwardly, unable to speak, the cabinet clutched to her breast like a stricken child.

In her bedroom she carried the beautifully-polished cabinet with the long, delicate legs to a shadowed corner away from the window, the door, and any other furniture. She did not understand this impulse exactly; she just felt the need to isolate the cabinet, to protect it from any other element in her previous life in this house. Because somehow she already knew that her life after the arrival of this delicate assemblage of different shades of wood would be a very different affair.

Once she had the cabinet positioned as seemed appropriate—based on some criteria whose source was completely mysterious to her—she sat on the edge of her bed and watched it until it was time to go downstairs and help the cook prepare dinner for her husband. Afterwards she came back and sat in the same position, gazing, and singing softly to herself for two, three, four hours at least. Until the sounds in the rest of the house had faded. Until the soft amber glow of the new day appeared in one corner of her window. And until the stirrings inside the cabinet became loud enough for her to hear.

She came unsteadily to her feet and walked across the rug with her heart racing, blood rushing loudly into her ears. She held her breath, and when the small voice flowered on the other side of the shiny cabinet wall, she opened its tiny door.

Twenty years after his wife's death, Jacob entered her bedroom for the third and final time. The first time had been the afternoon he had strode in to announce his well-meant but inadequate gift to her. The second time had been to find her lifeless body sprawled on the rug when she had failed to come down for supper. And now this third visit, for reasons he did not fully understand, except that he had been overcome with a terrible sadness and sense of dislocation these past few weeks, and this dusty bed chamber was the one place he knew he needed to be.

He would have come before—he would have come a thousand times before—if he had not been so afraid he could never make himself leave.

He had left the room exactly as it had been on Alma's last day: the covers pulled back neatly, as if she planned an early return to bed, a robe draped across the back of a cream-upholstered settee, a vanity table bare of cosmetics but displaying an antique brush and comb, a half-dozen leather-bound books on a shelf mounted on the wall by her window. In her closet he knew he would find no more than a few changes of clothes. He didn't bother to look because he knew they betrayed nothing of who she had been. She had lived in this room as he imagined nuns must live, their spare possessions a few bare strokes to portray who they had been.

It pained him that it was with her as it had been with everyone else in his life—some scattered sticks of furniture all he had left to remember them by—where they had sat, what they had touched, what they had held and cared for. He had always made sure that when some member of the family died he got something, any small thing, they had handled and loved, to take back here to watch and listen to. And yet none was haunted, not even by a whisper. He knew—he had watched and listened for those departed loved ones most of his adult life.

His family hadn't wanted him to marry her. No good can come, they said, of a union with one so strange. And though he had loved his family, he had separated from them, aligning himself with her in this grand house away from the staring eyes of the town. It had not been a conventional marriage—she could not abide being touched and permitted him to see her only at certain times of the day, and even then he might not even be present as far as she was concerned, so intent was she on her conversation with the people and things he could not see.

His family virtually abandoned him over his choice, but as a grown man it was his choice to make. He was never sure if his beloved Alma had such choices. Alma had been driven, apparently, by whatever stray winds entered her brain.

The gift she had chosen in lieu of a child (for how could he give his child such a mother, or give his wife such a tender thing to care for?) still sat in its corner in shadow, appearing to lean his way on its insubstantial legs. He perceived a narrow crack in the front surface of the small cabinet, which drew him closer to inspect the damage, but it was only that the small door was ajar, inviting him to secure it further, or to peek inside.

Jacob led himself into the corner with his lantern held before him, and grasping the miniature knob with two trembling fingers pulled it away from the frame, and seeing that the door had a twin, unclasped the other side and spread both doors like wings that might fly away with this beautiful box. He stepped closer then, moving the light across the cabinet's interior like a blazing eye.

The inside was furnished like some doll's house, and it saddened him to see this late evidence of the state of Alma's thinking. Here and there were actual pieces of doll furniture, perhaps kept from her girlhood or "borrowed" from some neighbour child. Then there were pieces—a settee very like the one in this room, a high-backed Queen Anne chair—carved, apparently, from soap, now discoloured and furred by years of clinging dust and lint.

Other furniture had been assembled from spools and emery boards, clothespins, a small jewellery box, then what appeared to be half a broken drinking cup cleverly upholstered with a woman's faded black evening glove.

He was surprised to find in one corner a small portrait of himself, finely painted in delicate strokes, and one of Alma set beside it. And underneath, in tiny, almost unreadable script, two words, which he was sure he could not read correctly, but which might have said "Father", "Mother".

He decided he had been hearing the breathing for some time—he just hadn't been sure of its nature, or its source. The past few years he had suffered from a series of respiratory ailments, and had become accustomed to hearing a soft, secondary wheeze, or leak, with each inhalation and exhalation of breath. That could easily have been the origin of the sounds he was hearing.

But he suspected not. With shaking hand he reached into the far corner of the box, where a variety of handkerchiefs and lacy napkins lay piled. He peeled them off slowly, until finally he reached that faint outline beneath a swatch of dress lace, a short thing curled onto itself, faintly moving with a laboured rasp.

He could have stopped then, and thought he should, but his hand was moving again with so little direction, and just nudged that bit of cloth, which dropped down a bare quarter inch.

Nothing there, really, except the tiny eyes. Tissue worn to transparency, flesh vanished into the dusty air, and the child's breathing so slight, a parenthesis, a comma. Jacob stared down solemnly at this kind afterthought, shadow of a shadow, a ghost of a chance. Those eyes so innocent, and yet so old, and desperately tired, an intelligence with no reason to be. Dissolving. The weary breathing stopped.

In the family plot, what little family there might be, there by Alma's grave he erected a small stone: "C. Child" in bold but fine lettering. There he buried the cabinet and all it had contained, because what else had there been to bury? Two years later he joined them there, on the other side.

The Still, Cold Air

Russell took possession of his parents' old house on a cold Monday morning. The air was like a slap across his cheeks. The frost coating the bare dirt yard cracked so loudly under his boots he looked around to see if something else had made the sound. Nothing grew here but a few large trees. His parents had left behind an old washer, a scattering of junk-filled cans and buckets, the front grill of an old Chevrolet, and some mouldy, unidentifiable bit of taxidermy. A set of rusted bulkhead doors probably led to the basement. He hadn't wanted the property, and his sisters didn't want him to have it.

"You don't deserve their house, you know," Angela had said, before handing him the keys. "You hated them, didn't you? I mean what else could it be the way you treated them? You must have hated them."

And of course he didn't deserve it. He'd been estranged from them his entire adult life, but he didn't have much choice. Winter was here, and he'd been living out of his car the last three months. Did he hate them? He actually had no idea. The bigger question was why they had willed him their house.

The key was giving him trouble—he examined it— worn thin and scratched up, the lock itself fairly chewed up as well. He eased the key in carefully, feeling for a fit, afraid he was going to snap it. Snow hadn't actually started yet, but tiny bits of ice floated in the air, now and then landing with a sting. Not a good night to spend in the car, especially with his own house at hand, however shabby and worn down. He tilted his head back and looked up at the sky—it wasn't just a snow sky, but a sky on the verge of imminent collapse. The roof line drooped directly above him, the eaves tipped back with the corners sagging even lower. From the street the grey roof looked like an old woman's floppy, misshapen hat, with some fat animal hidden inside to make it bulge along one side. He recognised his father's repair system in that—why replace a broken ceiling joist when you could wrap wire around it or nail on extra scraps of wood to strengthen it or tie it to a roof rafter? The result was that runaway warping as the other roof members generated torque around his amateur repairs. It was a wonder the whole thing hadn't already come crashing down, or some passing inspector hadn't stopped in alarm and condemned the place. The front door suddenly gave way and he stumbled inside.

It opened into the living room, which seemed to be not much warmer than the outside. He flipped on the light and looked around for the thermostat. He had no idea how he was going to pay for heat and electricity. But even if the utility company shut off the power it was still better than living out of his car. Maybe his sisters would help out. Unlikely, but possible.

He could see very little bare wall in the living room. Large book cases with books jammed in vertically, horizontally, and all angles in between took up most of the area. Much of the remaining wall space was hung with large rugs and woven pieces, and battered overstuffed chairs had been pushed against them, with quilts and towels and blankets and even old clothes wadded behind and in every available space between the furniture. He pulled out a heavy chair and removed the miscellaneous cloth shoved behind it. There was a gap of about two inches between the wall and the floor with frigid air—he guessed from the basement—pouring out. He shoved this insulation back into place as quickly as he could and walked around the perimeter of the room, occasionally getting down on his hands and knees to inspect what his parents had done to block the drafts. In spots wads of cloth had actually been taped or glued. He stood up and looked at the ceiling—the surface was uneven, dipping and rolling as he scanned from one side to the other, and two of the taller bookcases had been jammed into place to support it. He didn't dare move anything for fear the entire jerry-rigged arrangement would collapse on him.

The wind groaned and whistled on the other side of the door, softly whining through unplugged passages. The walls appeared to shake. The cold found his spine, and brushed up his vertebrae, playing with his nerves.

He understood now why his sisters didn't want the house. What he didn't understand was why they'd been so displeased he'd gotten it. He would have thought they'd find it suitable punishment for his sins, but perhaps his parents hadn't told them everything.

"We're not asking for any money, son. Just some physical help so that I can fix a few things. That's all." His father had sounded frail on that first of numerous calls. Russell almost thought the old man was faking it. But that voice, it sounded—what was the word—shredded?

"No time, Dad," he'd said, although most days it was a struggle just coming up with things to do. "Ask the girls. If not them, they have husbands."

There was a long pause at the other end. "They'd worry too much. They live too far away and I know they'd drop everything, disrupt their lives . . . " He stopped awhile, coughed uncontrollably. "It wouldn't be fair. You live less than a hundred miles away." His mother's voice rose in the background, garbled, indistinct. "Wait a minute, okay?" When he came back he said, "We don't have much, but we'd pay you for your time, feed you, whatever you need."

"I'm pretty busy, Dad, like I said. Look, I'll call you back." He'd called back two days later. "Just can't do it, Dad. What was that you used to say? 'You'll have to figure this one out for yourself.' When I was in jail?" Russell couldn't remember which particular jail term it had been, but that advice had been standard issue for the old man. He hung up, but before he did, he couldn't be sure, but he thought the old guy had been crying.

One of the bookcases had a hole punched through the back to access the thermostat mounted on the wall behind it. He finally heard the furnace fan screech on.

A tour of the rest of the house required but a few minutes. One door went to a dull green bedroom large enough for a full bed and dresser. A square panel in the ceiling provided access to the attic. One day he would check to see how bad it was up there. A narrow path around the bedroom wall led to the house's only bathroom, large enough for one person to stand in, use the toilet or bathe. The porcelain displayed a dull patina of rust stain. Another door off the living room took him into a tiny kitchen with a chipped yellow table.

This was what his parents had moved into after all their resources dried up. What happened to most of their belongings? Maybe they'd been stuffed into basement and attic for more homemade insulation.

He walked to the living room window, showering himself with enormous grey clots of dust as he pulled back the curtain. The new snow had filled the grassless yard quickly, catching in the limbs of the skinny bare trees until they overflowed and leaned. It tumbled out of the sky like rapidly disintegrating hospital linen. He hadn't visited his parents in the hospital. Angela said they'd barely made it through the night after the train went through their car. He'd travelled over that crossing less than a block away to reach this shabby cul-de-sac.

The dense white air sparked with random headlight reflections. He pressed one cheek against the biting glass and looked up through the dark in order to see the edge of the elevated highway a few dozen yards distant. A large truck swung top-heavy and sideways perilously close to the edge of the floating ribbon of dirty concrete, wheels thundering beneath the panicked horn. He imagined he could feel the quieting snow attempt to absorb the sound. His cheek began to numb and his face to twitch before he peeled it away from the pane and pulled the curtain snugly over the night.

As Russell turned around a moment's disorientation made him close his eyes. The effect of the frigid window lingered on his cheek. He raised his hand to rub his face and momentarily lost his balance, opening his eyes with a start. The living room seemed smaller than it had before, as if the intense cold had contracted the walls. That must be an effect of the unfamiliarity of the place. But a small place seemed even smaller if you'd lived in it a number of years as his parents had, as he had in his last apartment. He remembered thinking he'd do anything for just a couple of more square feet. Some days his apartment had felt like nothing more than a tight and clunky, smelly suit he'd been forced to wear. It had embarrassed him to live there.

A cold line glided across his wrist and lingered there, as if it were an absent finger seeking contact. He tensed, waiting for something more but it did not come. He held out his arm like a divining rod and walked helplessly in circles, seeking the source of the cold, feeling led and teased.

He hadn't even noticed that the furnace fan had stopped whining after awhile. He walked over by the heat grate low in the wall. Air hot as flame shot out, carrying long spongy strands of dust like snake spirits. He watched entranced as they first hung up on the grate then spun loose and floated around the room. He'd have to change the filter soon.

He didn't completely trust the already-made bed, but he no longer had sheets of his own. In the car he'd slept in layers of underwear, sweaters, bathrobe, and three coats. The sheets and blankets looked clean enough, but they had that old man smell. More cells dying, and the lungs working harder to push in and out the stale air. He supposed one day he would also smell that way.

He considered turning the heat down before bed, switching off the lights. But heat and lights were a luxury he wished to bathe in.

A sheet had been draped over the small bedside table. Removing it he discovered a small thirteen inch TV; by manoeuvring the coat hanger jammed into the broken aerial he acquired a fuzzy picture, but no sound. For a few minutes he watched a rolling image of a weatherman walking around outside against a sky filled with snow and static. Now and then the static would leak out of the sky and fill the entire frame. He assumed the broadcast was local, but on days like this it was easy to imagine the whole world snowing.

He flipped the set off and settled in. The bed was freezing, the bedroom heat vent broken or clogged. The pillow felt hard, cold and greasy against his neck, a refrigerated pig. He didn't care. He closed his eyes, expecting fatigue and body heat to solve all his problems.

From his nights in his car he naturally fell into a kind of half-sleep. He was vaguely cognisant of a glow from the snow filling the world outside, pushing through the curtains, bathing the interior of the undersized house with its blue-white persistence. He needn't go to a window or open a door to see the increasing accumulation; he could feel it coming down, out of the distant dark and through his half-sleep and covering the dirty, disappointing city, filling this cul-de-sac with swollen empty dreams and erasing the grimiest details. He suffered the weight of it; half hoping it would either kill him or put him unconscious, it scarcely mattered which. He heard the creaking overhead and, sleepily aware of the increasing mass on the malformed roof, he found himself smiling. But although the roof groaned and the walls trembled and sighed, the pitiful structure held, at least for now.

For now but wait but wait the words dropped into his ears and stayed. They did not bring him fully awake but they made him consider. Two voices fighting for dominance, and vaguely familiar.

In the distant other side of sleep he heard wind gusts under the eaves, pushing against brittle siding. The house stirred but he did not. Waited and waited until there was no hope, whispered with bitter control; he considered he might be in a struggle with his shoulders, trying not to hear. He felt a memory of light warming his eyelids, trying to make him raise them, but he would not.

Then thunder in his head as he fought the suspect sheets that once enshrouded the old couple who'd raised him—And You Left Us Here Alone!

Russell tore the bed clothing from his chest and neck, desperate to breathe. He thought he might have called out—at least he was confident he'd heard a voice so like his own on either this side or the other of the heavy curtains. The bed clothes slid away and off the bed like a sudden failure of skin. He was now cold to his bones and scrambled frantically to drape himself again.

Sounds were muted. He felt curled into the centre of a cocoon of hush. Outside the wind slipped off the roof and tumbled. He imagined he could hear the sound of noiseless footsteps creating a progression of holes through the snow and halting outside his window, the depressions filling with shadow.

He eased himself across the bed and pulled a bit of curtain off the window. Nothing peered in but an oval pattern of rime centred on the pane. Through the empty holes for eyes and mouth he could see the wobble of restless foliage. The wind coughed up billows of powdered snow, walked them across the drifted lawn and abandoned them to the ice-laden streets. In distant neighbourhoods the yellow lights blinked and smeared.

The phone rang out jangled and upset. Russell hadn't even known there was a phone, hadn't seen it, and certainly hadn't authorised its connection. But it called out from somewhere within the room. He crawled over the cluttered floor, brushing books, papers, clothes or rags away with the gross movement of hands and arms, swinging and batting in an urgency to kill the obnoxious sound. His fingers brushed the receiver and he jerked it up to his ear.

"Yes . . . " he answered, as if about to be ordered to do something he wanted no part of.

"Russell?" He thought it was one of his sisters, but he didn't know which one. "Are they there? If they are you must let them in. Do you appreciate . . . how cold . . . " The connection filled with waves of static which washed through the receiver and across his chilled arm.

"Angela? Beth?" But there was no answer, and he didn't bother calling out his other sisters' names. Who was coming? And in this weather? He dropped the phone.

Something smacked against the window, flat and unpadded. Russell thought of the unlikely possibility of a bare hand, ungloved, unprotected. His sisters were foolish that way. A trip involving at least three of them, come here to complain or intervene (all under the guise of "helping"), had always been a prospect. Maybe there were things of value still hidden in the house, although he couldn't imagine where, and they wanted their portion. It never paid to underestimate people's greed, even family members'.

There was a chuffing sound outside, like someone struggling through the snow. Or it might have been a panting dog in the next room. Interrupted sleep caused a corruption of the senses, so he could trust his own perceptions no more than the good will of others. But there was that chuffing sound again, a mouth seeking oxygen perhaps, but all it got for its efforts was a throat full of cold. He grabbed for the phone again and dragged it to his ear. The line was still open, with a steady train of distant, oft-repeated soft explosions of air, like a life stuttering out of the world. He laid the receiver gently back into the cradle, not wanting to make a sound, not wanting to encourage any sort of response. Someone wept, either outside the house or inside these poor walls, or inside his head. But he couldn't allow them to freeze, at least not here.

Russell climbed to his feet, feeling around on his body, attempting to bring it to life. He'd gone to bed in his clothes; he didn't own pajamas. He was grateful, but after searching the room in the dim light leaking around the edge of curtain he couldn't find his boots, and he was reluctant to turn on the light. The space under the bed was jammed with plastic bags. He put several over each foot, attempted to tie them into place.

The living room smelled of warm furnace dust and air breaking down into something darker and less useful. He opened the front door slowly and, closing his eyes briefly, let the cold air rush him into its embrace. Sighing, he looked around at the drifts, now a foot high and creeping taller against the house. It should stay this way, he thought, the downy white having transformed the grungy yard into a painting. He recognised a hulking phantom of snow and ice as his car. But the automobile seemed strangely past, a useless memory. One large tree appeared to have given up against the weight of snow and now leaned dangerously close. He saw no signs of his sisters, but he could see the holes they'd made in the snow, the wind not quite having erased their footprints. He heard them whispering, or whimpering around the side of the house. It served them right if they'd gotten themselves into trouble, but he couldn't just leave them there.

The plastic bags kept the damp out, but the lack of boots made him unsteady on his feet. He teetered this way and that, rocking his body through the snow, his view skewed by imbalance. The snow smelled of air cleansed of human contact. The roof loomed, parts sagging with incompetent support. He found himself staring at the perimeter of the eaves, the edges of the windows. Balls and ovals of ice clung there, as if whispers and open-mouthed cries had crusted over, hard ice expressions with hollow lament trapped inside.

A sudden gust of wind picked up with rapid feminine tittering, blew it around the house until the voices became a glacial mist. He arrived too late, the only signs were the curved icicles clawing the edges of the metal basement hatch.

The stuck front door panicked him until he slammed it open with a thrust of shoulder and thigh. He staggered in, the moonlight gathering around him to illuminate the impoverished state of the room. His parents had left him everything, and nothing. He forced the door shut, hearing the splintering as the bottom pushed on the threshold covered with intruding snow. He was still able to latch it, but the effort made him weepy.

The phone was ringing in the bedroom. He stumbled in, sat down on the edge of the unsteady bed and picked it up. The line was dead, the receiver icy against his ear as he listened to the cold empty air. "With no signal, nothing comes across," he thought he said aloud.

In the darkened room he felt the bitter air moving around him. The old house leaked, and he should never have accepted it. As he raised his head and stared at nothing, the shadows began to rearrange. All those years he had successfully kept his distance. He felt so frozen, and all he wanted was not to feel at all. The small house sighed, and then it trembled, and now it seemed no larger than the confines of his head.

He should never have gone out. He should never have come here in the first place. If he had more time maybe he could figure things out, even though figuring things out had never been his strong suit. He'd made so many bad mistakes. And now in the still, cold air he realised he'd let them in.

G is for Ghost

The architect had engaged Lewis to gut a house near the middle of Crisscross Row. The clients were young marrieds, double-income with no kids. Dinks. He'd done a number of these: the couple would buy some old Victorian because of the glamour of it, the grace, but before moving in they'd have the interior scooped out and hauled away, then replaced it with a condominium-style décor, probably not much different from the one they lived in now. It was crazy, but Lewis got paid for demolition, not psychiatry.

The house had twin gables out front and ornamented gutters. The outside lights and the lightning rods up on the roof had filigree work around the bases. Finely detailed gingerbread braced the eaves. The paint had been kept up: there was very little chipping and the shingles looked intact. A couple of clapboards showed some splitting, but there didn't seem to be any water damage. The garden around the side still bore flowers, and the driveway leading up to a separate, finely-kept garage, was a smooth, unbroken stretch of clean concrete.

The other houses on the block were similarly well-kept. Closely-trimmed grass, shaped hedges and shrubs, lots of shiny glass. All the garbage cans disguised as planters or hidden behind their own fences. No ugly sisters on this block. There wouldn't be much turnover in residences here; most everybody would be pretty well established.

Lewis usually didn't find much work in neighbourhoods like these. He wondered if the well-to-do young couple would be welcomed here.

If they actually moved in, of course. In more than one of these projects the young couple had backed out. If they had the money, he supposed they felt they could afford to be fickle. But usually not before the house had already been autopsied, all its insides gone forever.

The architect had given him a plan and a grocery list of what had to go. That was the common procedure. Sometimes the buyer would come by to watch some of the demolition, but that usually wasn't the case. Most didn't want to watch; they kept their distance, dealing exclusively through the architect or some contractor. Lewis dealt a lot with people who liked to maintain their distance: chief architects who didn't even want a glance at the property until the greater part of the dirty work had been done; young buyers whose interest stayed remote and general until he'd removed a ton of old plaster and lathe from the place; all kinds who didn't like the grime of what he had to do to someone's grand old memories. And maybe memory was part of the key. The houses they had bought—and he had to gut—were so like houses remembered from childhood, or from dreams of childhood. But now all the cosy furniture's been moved out and the people have died or moved away and only the grizzled memories remained.

It reminded him of those old-fashioned ghost stories where the storyteller keeps you at a supposedly safe distance by telling you that he heard the tale from a friend of a friend, or read about it in a letter or a diary written by someone who lived a century before. And it does make you feel a little more secure for a while. But then the very distance of the telling makes you think terrible things might happen to just about anyone. You're too far away from the ghost to see the wires that make it glide. Then you begin to wonder if the author feels he has to tell it to you at such a distance because your nerves might unravel if exposed too closely to this awful manifestation. The ghosts in such stories were like most people's memories: in order for them to function normally these spectres had to be kept at a distance, but keeping these spectres at a distance made them all the more awful—more awful because they began to seem less and less a part of you.

Lewis understood the need, all right; it was always a gamble. He'd lost a mother, a wife, and a daughter not yet three in a house very much like this one—his whole life burned to smoke the shape of his memories. After ten years, and the pain of the grief being no better, his doctor had him write down the most important of these memories on separate sheets of paper, then burn them one at a time in an ashtray. It had seemed an atrocity at first, until he realised that the memories were still there—the act had just made it seem possible that there was room for the new as well. Like these houses. He might scrape them clean to the outside walls like some crude gynaecologist, but the grey phantoms of the lives that had begun and ended there would still be present, in his mind if in no other's.

Not that he'd ever believed in ghosts, at least not in the way people talked about them. Gnomes or gremlins or goblins or green gases guiding you through the hallways or something similar. He didn't understand any of that, none of it at all. He just knew that death wasn't as any of us had imagined it. Death was something we didn't know at all.

Maybe there was just too much of the grave in Lewis's work for the people who employed him. He'd stopped trying to figure, or to argue, or to suggest. He just did his job. He used to be a builder, back before he got the tremble in his hands. Now he was a destroyer. He did it quickly and efficiently, and always by himself. The fact was he didn't like people watching him while he did what he was paid to do.

He left the fancy gate wide open: he'd be going back and forth a lot and he didn't want to scratch it up. He could already feel the gazes at his back, the gatherings at windows all up and down Crisscross Row. He wanted them all to know that he was going to play the good guest on their block, and show this house the respect it deserved. If he was careful bringing the materials out to his truck, they'd hardly know what he was up to. Guilt warmed his face. Suddenly he felt like a ghoul.

The air inside the house was dry and slightly dusty. The electrician had left the power on to the main entrance hall—a bare bulb hung incongruously from a Gothic arch. Similar bulbs hung from strategic locations around the house. All remaining circuits had been cut, lifelines severed so that internal supports and sheathings could be safely removed. The shadowed walls had the serious, grim faces of corpses.

Lewis gestured vaguely to the house, as if delivering the last rites. He pulled his reciprocating saw out of its case, plugged it in and turned it on. Its high whine was like the garbled arguments of a thousand angry bees as he used it to gnaw through old plaster, lathe, and timber.

Lewis loved his houses and hated to see the old interiors go, but he had achieved enough distance through a range of demolition jobs that he always found things to appreciate as he unmade each house: a nail, a board, and a wall at a time. Once the dropped ceilings and floor coverings were taken away it was possible to trace the locations of older, non-bearing walls which had been removed during some previous remodelling.

The walls themselves most often clearly indicated the course of a house's evolution: layers of wallpaper and wallpaper borders tracking the changes in taste over generations, gas fixtures chopped off and their gaps plastered over, wires leading to a servant's bell, the shaft of an old dumb waiter, the pipes for a radiator system, knob and tube wiring, lost coins, lost toys, lost letters.

He found the yellowing sheets of paper wedged behind the baseboard of a small room at the back of the second floor. It had been a child's room several times during its lifetime; the third, fifth, and seventh layers of wallpaper all had a child's icons: teddy bears, dolls, toy soldiers. Even the original layer of plaster bore the crude, faded stencil of a hobbyhorse.

He unfolded the sheets carefully and settled down into a thin layer of plaster dust to read, gingerly—and soon reverently—turning the pages, reading about Jimmy.

☙

I thought the very casualness of it was going to push me over the edge.

Every day Jimmy did his usual things—getting up, getting dressed, eventually, fooling around before and after breakfast, and disappearing until school was out. After that, I could hear him outside, or in his room singing to himself. Occasionally, looking out my study window, I would catch a glimpse of his bright green jacket, his favourite piece of clothing.

But Jimmy had been dead just over a year.

I thought the very casualness of it was going to push me over the edge. Carol would just be talking about him, about something he had done or said that day, or talking to him, telling him he needed to clean his room before dinner or something, and I'd just have to get out of that room, I'd run crying out of that room, and Carol would just sit there—I thought—wondering what was the matter with me.

Today we were getting ready to drive up to Lookout Mountain. We were going to visit that spot near the top where Carol always piled oddly-shaped and coloured rocks in memory of him—he'd always loved rocks—his room was full of them and for days we kept finding them there and in odd places around the house when we finally faced the task of gathering up his things and cleaning out his room, scraping it hollow, to the very walls.

I didn't think we should take him up to the mountain. It seemed perverse. Carol was telling him to get that damn green coat on, to go get ready, we were leaving soon. And damned if he didn't leave the room singing, like we were all going on a picnic.

And I started crying. I never could cry right, and it leaked and spilled out of my eyes and all over me like a slow rupture of my head. She looked at me as if she were surprised. "What's wrong?" she said. For the first time since I'd known her, I could have slapped her.

"What if he doesn't know he's dead?" I cried. "Or if he's just a memory, and we're both crazy? Carol, don't we need to tell him? I don't know how we're going to tell him. I feel like I've failed him!"

She didn't say anything, and that infuriated me. She just gave me a quick hug and left the room. Maybe she didn't want the illusion, the glamour, spoiled. I don't know.

Suddenly Jimmy came into the room. I realised then I had never looked directly at him. I'd been too uncomfortable. And always before he'd appeared when Carol was with me, as if this were her experience, not mine; that she was the one responsible, and it was something I could only be embarrassed about. And underneath that feeling of embarrassment, such a terrible jealousy. But now my son had come to me, and so I thought I should look at him directly, look him in the eyes.

He was pale, whiter than I remembered, and grey when he stepped through shadow. But not so pale, not so pale after all. My own skin had taken on this alabaster colour. In the past year I'd hardly been outside the house.

I made myself pick him up. I made myself hold him. That peculiar warm, clean smell of his hair filled me— it was a smell that would be with me, I knew, forever. I thought about how we were going to tell him, finally, how the bedtime stories might be changed, altered slightly, to prepare him, how a bedtime story might be the best way to tell him that he was dead, to tell us that he was dead.

I squeezed him, tighter to me, then held back, suddenly afraid that I might squeeze right through him.

"I love you," I said, and began to cry. "I love you . . . very much."

After a time of holding, and kissing, and whispering secrets I'd almost, but not quite, forgotten, I felt the gentle outline of his small hand pressing into my back, holding me.

And passing through. And passing through. And passing . . .

૭૦

The words trailed off the edge of the page, as if the paper couldn't hold them within its bounds. Lewis wondered about how many families ago this family had been, how many lives ago. He wondered where that mother was, and what had happened to that father, and if the son still played here on long hot summer afternoons, and if he were warm enough when ice caked the windows, and the cold was a snake looking for a gap in the framing for its slow passage into the house.

The dust rose and settled in the room, sunlight making it glitter as it drifted past his face and out the door. And when he finally stood with crowbar in hand and swung it in tight arcs into the walls, a smell of warm hair and a grin the length of a boy's forgotten name came up to greet him.

Breaking the Rules

Again Raymond peered through the curtains of the front window. Again he made sure the door was bolted. If he could see Mary before she actually stepped up on to their front porch then perhaps he'd have some unspecified advantage over her. He'd never seen this belief recorded, nor heard it from any of the soiled derelicts he regularly consulted two blocks away, but it made sense. You never knew when you might stumble across one of the valid rules of the universe.

No sign of her. But of course it was still much too early. He checked the bolt on the door. There were always others who might take advantage of her arrival to sneak past him. He reminded himself that when she finally did arrive he needed to make sure that she crossed the threshold with her right foot first. He didn't know exactly how he was going to orchestrate this; perhaps he could stop her as she entered, claiming a weakness in the floor, and guide her across with a hand on her arm and his toe nudging the proper foot.

The empty sky above the buildings across the street had grown overcast, and the smudge was spreading down the buildings themselves and into the oily pavement that fronted their little home. Lightning flashed suddenly behind a crack in the clouds. The universe was smiling at him.

Raymond smiled back, as if privy to the joke. Best to keep up a good front. It was not as if he were superstitious.

He had always tried to be reasonable. It only made sense that some of those thousands of odd beliefs expressed valid, working rules. If you assumed that the universe had rules—for gravity, for speed, for safety, for luck—and hadn't modern science proved this?

But there seemed to be no systematic way to determine which of the rules were valid. It finally occurred to him that if he followed all of the beliefs, then success was inevitable, for the valid rules would function as desired, and the invalid rules would have no effect at all. However, he had to avoid such contradictory convictions as the beliefs that black cats were both good and bad luck. He checked the door again. The bolt was still in place.

Raymond stared out the window for a time, watching the shadows deepen, some of them sprouting legs and walking by the house. Derelicts mostly, but now and then there would be a housewife, or a well-dressed workman with briefcase or lunchbox in hand. A figure swayed out of the shrubbery at the corner, its head three times normal, flattened on top so that the effect was like the profile of a soup bowl. Raymond drew back in alarm as the figure leaned forward as if searching the sidewalk for prey. But he wasn't surprised—not really. With all those careless people out in the city, breaking rules by the hour, some rather terrible aberrations were likely to evolve.

Then the light cast out from his window trapped the face and Raymond could see that it was the old lady from three houses down, her head unbalanced by a broad-brimmed hat.

He turned and gazed at the dark wood and faded Persian rug-covered steps of the staircase, straining to hear a sound which did not come. He smiled gratefully. He had disconnected his mother's bell—she might jab at her black button all night long and it would do her no good—but still he had almost expected its discordant jangle. She would blow up like a dark jellyfish if she knew he had another woman coming into their house. Or worse—a potential wife, a new life partner to help him sort out the rules. He smiled again and turned. The door was still locked. He smiled again. How many smiles per day would keep the loneliness away? He would have to make some calculations.

He had worked with Mary for several years. Actually, he was her immediate superior at the office, and she made very little money, but such things mattered little to him. Certainly a poor person knew as much about the secret rules of living as a rich person, perhaps more. A rich man could always buy his own good luck.

She was a pretty thing, but not so much as to attract undue attention. Raymond would hate that. If she was going to live under the same roof as his mother she would have to remain inconspicuous. Unusually beautiful or unusually ugly people tended to attract misfortune.

He went into the dining room to once again check the table settings. He had spent hours arranging and rearranging plates, bowls, cups, cutlery. He climbed up on one of the chairs and looked down at the table, framing it in his hands. He had experimented with the proximity of chairs and place settings, and made estimations concerning optimum personal space. In most cultures, of course, there was a definite point where the distance between two people engaged in conversation became intrusive and rude. The proper distance for encouraging intimacy also existed, he believed, but was much more difficult to pinpoint. He had padded Mary's chair so that he would be able to look into her eyes from a certain angle—at work he had calculated her height one day as she stood beside a filing cabinet. He glanced back at the door—the bolt was still in place.

He found himself staring at the tablecloth. Something wrong there, but he couldn't figure out what it was. He pondered the history of it, its past ownership. His mother's Aunt Betty had originally purchased it. No one of unusually bad fortune or disposition had ever owned the cloth, so there should be no problem. He gazed at the place settings, their precise spacing. The knives were antiques, iron. It had taken him a long time to find them. Protected you against witches and evil spirits, he'd heard. He chuckled to himself. If Mary was a witch she didn't stand a chance. He thought of his mother then, and hoped that Mary was a witch. He could do with a witch.

Then it came to him, the pattern floating up subtly from beneath the settings, the lines in the cloth so faint he'd almost not noticed them: a diamond-shaped crease at the centre of the tablecloth. A death omen. Raymond leapt off the chair and started pulling off the table settings. When he got down to the tablecloth he jerked it off unceremoniously and ran it out to the laundry room where he dumped it into a battered old hamper. He searched the cabinets frantically for a replacement and not finding one settled for an elegant linen bed sheet, the regular square folds in it all the better for a precise resetting of the table. He glanced at the door as he ran around the dining room, thinking that the bolt still looked latched but he couldn't be sure. He desperately wanted to go check it, to examine it physically, but the table had to be set before Mary arrived.

He was only halfway done when the bell rang. Startled, he gazed at the staircase, waiting for his mother to ring again. He thought he might scream, and then realised it was the front bell. He stumbled around the table and the plate in his hands slipped and crashed to the floor. Appalled, he looked down at the broken pieces. The bell rang again. He looked around quickly, spied an old worthless ceramic tea cup sitting on the sideboard, picked it up and smashed it on the floor in order to avoid another, more expensive breakage.

Raymond peeled the curtain back from the window and stared into the impatient face of his beloved. This was not going well at all. Behind Mary shadows stirred along the edges of the porch. Raymond hesitated as Mary looked at him with a puzzled expression. The shadows weaved drunkenly as Raymond struggled with the bolt. He could not free it. He made an uneasy grin at her through the glass. She looked ready to leave. The shadows heaved at the edges of the porch, gathering together for an assault. He couldn't possibly let her leave—she had no idea what dangers awaited her out there. You had to have a sense of order, a sense of the rules, else you faced the world completely without protection. If you didn't know the rules, danger had no face.

The bolt slid away and Raymond jerked open the door, reaching over the threshold (Was this wise? He couldn't remember) and grabbed Mary by the hand. Desperately he fell back, pulling her across and slamming the door before the shadows could leap.

"Mr. Jenks!" Mary sputtered, rubbing her hand. She looked at him warily. (Mr. Jenks? But I should be Raymond to you by now!) He stared at her feet—which had crossed first, the left or the right? He couldn't remember. Wind-blown shadows filled the door window as if mocking.

"I'm sorry, Mary. Terribly sorry." He looked around as if searching for something lost. "I fell, you see. Off balance, as I am . . . sometimes . . . " Mother's bell was ringing. Mary stared at him as if he were mad. He expected her to ask about the bell, but she did not.

"Oh . . . " She smiled slightly. "No harm done, I suppose." She looked past him, looking for the source of the bell? "Something smells wonderful. And the table so love-ly, I see. You've really gone all out." The smile grew larger, although slightly forced.

"Yes, yes," he said with mounting excitement, thinking she was his again. "You must sit down. Wouldn't do to let things get cold." (Cold?) He looked at her in embarrass-ment, hoping she didn't think he was making reference to her passion. But she seemed unaware. "Here . . . " He guided her toward the dining room, glancing back over his shoulder to make sure the bolt was latched again. "A moment . . . " He walked briskly back to the door and closed the curtain over the teeming shadows. He switched off the porch light, and then switched it on again. Then, reconsidering, he moved the switch up and down twice more. He turned and saw her puzzled expression. "Check-ing the operation . . . recent electrical problems, don't you know?" he mumbled quickly, and moved toward the din-ing room. How many times had he moved the switch? Now in his nervousness he could not remember. Dinner, at least, seemed to go according to plan. Roast beef of just the right tenderness so that he might see how she cut and how she chewed. Juicy, fresh-picked cherry tomatoes so that he might see how they fit between her lips, and whether she sucked, or tore the tender hearts out. Potatoes seasoned and baked until their stuffings virtually melted over her tongue. She ate well, but not too greedily, and he saw no evidence in her eating to suggest either the vixen or the harpy.

Then at dessert he narrowly avoided disaster. She in-sisted on going out to the kitchen to help serve the pud-ding. Obviously impressed with the kitchen's order and cleanliness, she'd remarked how "impressive" it was, "not at all what I'd expect in the kitchen of a bachelor living alone". He must have looked at her strangely, because what she had said frankly puzzled him, although he did not know why. She suddenly seemed uncomfortable with him. He grabbed her pudding off the counter and took it into the dining room where she started to sit in a different chair, not in the place he had originally set for her.

Raymond grabbed her arm at the last minute, too roughly he was sure. She winced and backed away from him. "Not that chair," he gasped. "It has a bad leg and might spill you." She smiled awkwardly and moved to her original setting, where she ate her soft dessert in silence.

Later during coffee, however, she placed her spoon with his in the same saucer—a promising omen of marriage to come if there ever was one. But then he realised she had just stirred the cream into her coffee counterclockwise. He waited with bated breath lest she complain of the drink's dreadful taste.

Now and then he would find some excuse to rise and recheck the bolted door and flip the light switch once, twice, then three, then four times for good measure. He laughed softly as he did so, as if this were all some joke, because he knew she was watching him closely now.

She offered to help with the dishes, of course, because she had been raised well. She again made some comment concerning "a man needing special help without a woman around", and again he was confused by this. He permitted her to help him in the kitchen even though, of all the rooms in a house, the kitchen was the one most fraught with danger.

While she put on his mother's apron he took the time to recheck the bolt on the front door and flip the light switch a few more times. He imagined he could hear the shadows moving back and forth across the porch, but he dared not peek else it might encourage their little joke. Passing the staircase he could have sworn he heard his mother's bell, but when he stopped it did not ring again.

As he re-entered the kitchen he saw Mary stooping to pick up the apron that had slipped off. He could feel the blood leaving his face as he raced to pick it up for her. "Don't you know what it can mean to drop an apron? How could you let this happen!" he shouted, and then felt sorry as she turned away in obvious embarrassment.

They worked in silence for a time before she said, still not looking at him, "I'm sorry, Mr. Jenks. You seem so impatient with me."

Without thinking he clutched at the towel in her hands. (A man and a woman should never dry on the same towel or a quarrel will surely follow.) "Drat, the towel! No, Mary . . . I couldn't be angry with you!"

"Mr. Jenks . . ."

"Jenks? Call me Raymond! Now that we've known each other so long . . ."

"But you're my boss. And it's only been six months." She was red-faced now, and he didn't think he could stand that after all his careful preparations, his meticulous observance of all the rules. He grabbed at her apron and rubbed his hands furiously into the stiff cloth. "There! I've wiped my hands on your apron, perfumed with your own potent perspiration. Don't you see? Now we're destined to be lovers!"

"Mr. Jenks!" she yelled, and started toward the back door off the kitchen.

"Mary, you little fool! Leave by the same door you entered or you'll take away all my luck with you!"

"You're crazy!" she threw back over her shoulder as she grabbed the knob and pulled. It would not budge. Raymond had nailed it shut long ago in anticipation of just such an unplanned, unfortunate exit.

She raced through a short hall toward the front door, the apron tangling about her feet so that she stumbled ("See!" he thought in triumph. "See what happens when the apron isn't tied securely?") and so Raymond was able to beat her to the door. He checked the bolt and flipped the light switch several times for good measure. He could sense the dark shadows on the other side of the door writhing in agony over his careful observance of rules and precautions. "Mary, sweet child, you can't fight the laws of the universe," he crooned. "None of us can. A little instruction on the proper observances, the necessary precautions, and you'll make me a wonderful wife! Not to worry, sweetheart. I'm quite a good teacher."

Mary spat at him ("Quick, what do I do with her phlegm?") and started scooting backward toward the staircase. "My brother . . . he's picking me up soon! Believe me, Mr. Jenks, you really wouldn't want to tangle with him!"

"I . . . don't . . . believe you," Raymond said with sudden strength of anger. He wanted to move toward her, but felt compelled instead to flip the light switch first, and wasn't this some universal instinct that might insure the success of his endeavour? So he flipped the porch switch once, twice, three times, then again and again, wanting to go to her and pick her up and yet wanting to flip that switch even more, revelling in the security of it, the sense of safety it brought him, as he flipped and flipped and flipped, eventually losing his precious count, but then not really caring as the light flashed and flashed and flashed across her sweet, vulnerable, stricken face.

"Leave me alone!" she shouted, racing up the stairs.

The sight of Mary heading up the staircase (into Mother's realm) made him pull his fingers away from the switch at last and pound up the stairs after her. Half-way up she stumbled on a stair and Raymond shrieked at the bad luck she continued to bring into his house, and then shrieked again when, worse still, in his haste he passed her. He grabbed her by the hair and jerked her to her feet roaring, "CAN YOU BEGIN TO IMAGINE HOW UNLUCKY THIS IS?"

And then there was the bell again, filling the house, taking the air, drowning out Mary's screams, pounding through Raymond's head.

"Mother! Can't you see I'm busy!" he shouted up the stairs.

On the other side of the front door a heaviness pressed and pounded on the panels and glass, calling Mary's name. Raymond decided that the shadows that had always been outside waiting for just this sort of opportunity were finally laying siege to the house. He began dragging Mary upstairs by her hair, determined to get her to safety before the grinning universe broke inside and swallowed them all.

He stopped and let go of Mary's hair. At the top of the stairs his mother stood grinning down at him (Raymond, you've brought this girl in here, you've broken all of my rules). He immediately began shuffling his feet against the nap of the rug that covered the staircase, trying to get it brushed in the right direction for his safe escape, but he could not remember what that right direction should be. He took one step up the staircase shuffle-shuffle, then one step backwards shuffle-shuffle-shuffle, and attempted to ignore all the screaming that surrounded him, cutting off his air. (Is the door locked? How many times did I flip the light switch?) For the life of him he could not remember.

There was a loud crash and seconds later hands clutched the backs of his shoulders, pulling him down the staircase and picking him up, shoving him, tossing him into the air and across the dining room table where he knocked the salt cellar across the room, spraying granules everywhere like so many spirits dying in the inhospitable air. He lay on the table ("Don't lie down on the table—you'll die within the year") staring at the evil omen of two crossed knives making a shiny X on the cloth in front of his nose.

("You left the ceramic animals facing the door, Raymond! I always told you that lets the luck run out of a house!") His mother's voice filled his ear, louder than all the others. He looked around at the knick-knack shelves in a daze. Mother was right, of course—they all seemed to be facing the door. Was the door well bolted? He could not remember.

"Let's get out of here, Sis," a low voice said from somewhere in the house. It could have been his father, but he could not remember what had ever happened to his father, except that it seemed his father had never really understood the rules of the world.

"Wait . . . wait," Raymond said weakly, struggling to sit up on the table. "I've been impolite. I should have introduced you to my mother." He gestured toward the top of the stairs.

"Come on, Sis. The guy's crazy . . . "

"Mr. Jenks . . . " Mary's sweet voice floated out of the teeming shadows closing in around him, grinning at him. "Isn't your—but I heard your mother was dead."

Raymond started laughing, sharing in the shadows' joke. "But I broke the rules," he said. "I knew she was dying, and I was supposed to leave the windows open, you see, so that she might have an easy passage to heaven." He chuckled. "But I was afraid of all those people outside, just waiting for me to slip up so that they could get inside. And besides, it was so cold that month. So I kept all the windows closed. She died, you see, and the windows were closed. Closed and locked."

He began laughing in earnest then, and could not stop. He tumbled off the table and laughed some more. He checked the front door bolt, and laughed wildly at the shattered state of it. He turned the porch light off and on, off and on, and off and on, laughing all the while.

He ran through his mother's house unveiling all the mirrors he'd covered the night his mother died. He stared at his reflection in each one, laughing, waiting for his own dying to begin, and his grinning reflection to disappear.

How many minutes of laughter will ensure a place in hell? He'd have to do some calculations.

The Slow Fall of Dust
in a Quiet Place

When I was a child my mother read to me daily, from whatever texts she might access. One of these was a series of articles about a hermit who used to live in our town. "I feel more comfortable with absences," he was quoted as saying, as if that explained anything. And, of course, it did. For even then I knew what he meant. Far better to choose an absence than to have an absence forced upon you. When the hermit died the town discovered that he had left a great deal of money for the construction of a children's park. The articles quoted several townspeople who talked about what a beloved figure this man had been. My mother told me that this simply was not true—very few people had even known the man, and only a small percentage of those had found him to be anything other than unpleasant. No one had seen any evidence of how he felt about children. But they still named the new park after him, and people forever after would think of him as a nice man.

Very few have seen any evidence of my feelings for children, but this does not mean I do not have them. Simply because I treasure my quiet times does not mean I am a cold fish. Not a very original phrase, mind you, and one that I would not care to use myself, but Martha seemed to enjoy the sound of it. Saying it slowly, carefully, so that it sounded like a wet breeze through the trees outside.

This house has always creaked and wept and sung, especially when my family was here. I do not pretend to understand the physics of such things, but I have lived in old houses before, and the combination of loose boards, warped timbers, and dust accumulation does appear to create an environment in which sounds travel along strange paths throughout a house, and ancient iron has been known to sweat, and vocalise, and impart to water an odd or forbidding taste. Faulty wiring may cause lights to dim and blink. Doors fall open without provocation. Even on the hottest day of the year there may be a draft rattling my papers and chilling the flesh of my arms. I suppose I should be thankful, actually. This responsive architecture has saved me from feeling completely alone.

But still, I cannot shake the feeling that these small daily events are a judgment against me.

I have always preferred a slow, measured movement of things, and people. I have always preferred a quiet place in which to read and think. This does not mean I do not like other people. This does not mean I cannot love.

The comfort in routine is sometimes difficult to explain to the young. My morning tea. My morning toast. The way I carry them each day in the same cup, the same saucer, down the moaning steps into my basement full of books. There I hold my cup or my toast in one hand while wiping the books with a large red cloth in the other. The cloth is first sprayed with my own mixture of light oils and water: nothing that will damage the books, mind you, just the right blend for ridding them of dust.

In the beginning I used a feather duster. Goose feathers, I believe they were, but soon I realised that only rearranged the dust, reduced the build-up on particular surfaces, sent it flying through the dim basement air so that it might redistribute itself on other surfaces. You cannot solve a problem simply by relocating it, my mother used to say. So much wisdom I've failed to appreciate in my lifetime, until long after the speakers were dead.

My daughter never did understand this need for dusting. Nor did she appreciate the importance of my routine. I tried my best to spare her feelings, as any father would, but I could not tolerate her interruptions.

Dust is persistent. Dust clings and builds, falls and then clings again. Dust is created with every movement of our bodies, every friction, every handling, every gesture, every expression. Dust travels and dust waits, and resists all attempts to erase. So to maintain at least the illusion of cleanliness, the vaguest notion of control, I wipe as many of my books as possible each morning with the rag, then throw the rag in the wash immediately, counting on the power of this ancient plumbing to carry all that dust away. Only then do I feel comfortable beginning my reading, or my correspondence, or my list of activities for the day.

For dust destroys, you see. It is the very embodiment of all that troubles us about the past: its filth, its squalor, and its complications. Books sour under the weight of its accumulation. And I have been dismayed to see that with my wife gone, my daughter gone, there is even more dust than ever before.

When we first moved into this house twenty years ago my books had not yet arrived from New England. They were delayed several weeks, in fact, and for the first time in my memory I spent an extended period without books to read. We only had a little money at the time—my job as proofreader for a banknote printer had only just begun— and Martha's teacher's salary would not be paid for a week or so. So instead of buying a quantity of reading material whose permanent status within my collection might be in doubt, I bought newspapers and a few magazines whose disposability was well-established. I moved in one of our large Queen Anne wingbacks and read from a stack of newsprint kept in a cardboard box beside me. It was a very different experience for me, and not an entirely unpleasant one. There is a certain comfort in openness, in possibilities not yet realised or even fully contemplated. My basement office could hold an unimaginable variety and quality of content because, as yet, it held none.

I often miss that openness, the cleanliness of that kind of lifestyle. I have far too many things to think about and remember. Far too many sounds and whispers to contend with.

Arranging the books when they finally arrived was a real pleasure, of course. Devising yet another new classification system, rediscovering volumes I'd forgotten I had, reading scattered passages in various books and then laying them aside like nibbled sandwiches. Attempting to describe my relationship with my books makes me sound a bit odd and obsessive, I know, very much the eccentric young man become the socially awkward old man, but I am not alone in my illness. So many of us have better relationships with our things than with the people in our lives.

Perhaps I should explain my choice of a basement for my books and documents, certainly not the most hospitable environment for paper. It was Martha's idea. Martha was always a great person of ideas. I greatly admired ideas, of course, whoever might be the author. But I had very few of my own.

So during those first few weeks in the new house I sat amid the richness of vacancy and read of crimes and opinions, current fashions and business trends, the occasional sad story meant to stir someone else to action. Upstairs, in the living portion of the house, Martha brought in a parade of contractors to carpet and glaze and relocate doorways, windows, and walls. As structures which had not been disturbed in decades were brought to ruin or into the context of some new plan, dust—equally aged in decades—was released, forced out, put into flight, until it eventually fell, drifted, settled into the lowest point of the house, which was my basement sanctuary.

It was quite an interesting phenomenon to watch, actually, sitting in my greying reading chair. Even when work was being done on the second story, or far up in the attic, dust managed eventually to make its way down to me. If the light through the grimed basement windows was of the proper angle I might even see the journey of individual particles of dust, drifting slowly down from the dark masses above, like a slow fall of minute skeletons through unexplored reaches of ocean.

So it was I felt compelled to begin my routine of dusting even before my books had arrived. And after, it seemed absolutely necessary to stave the tide of everything I owned and cared about from being transformed into trash.

But only saints, madmen, and bachelors seem able to maintain their routines over extended periods of time. I had never planned to have children. They were not a part of my imagined life. And certainly this was not because I dislike them. I could not begin to count the number of times I have shed tears over the death of a child in a book or play. Or felt an unplanned-for smile playing with my lips upon reading some description of their antics. I was never a child hater, as my wife had accused me. To be honest she said this only once, but even a single such accusation is too much to be borne. I will never forgive her for that. She was horribly wrong. I loved my daughter and the great pain of my life is that I know she loved me.

Despite my misgivings Martha wanted a child, and like any good husband I acceded to her wishes. This was not an easy process for me. Frankly, I had always felt a little foolish about sexual matters, and the constraints and obsessiveness over timing imposed by Martha's rather fragile fertility exacerbated my awkwardness. But I loved my wife. I would love my child. At the very least it was what Martha demanded, and I always respected my wife's demands.

Please do not misunderstand me. After she was born, I loved my baby, my Kat (again, Martha's idea, but I eventually warmed to the name). I could not help myself. I tried to keep my distance at first, supposing that this was what Martha wanted. But with each rustle, faint protesting cry, minute disturbance of the bedclothes, I'd go trotting over to her crib. Not that I had any idea what to do. Sometimes I'd place my forefinger on her plump little arm and mutter "there there", fearing all the time that I might break something. Usually I'd stand two steps back, calling Martha or the nanny to please come and do something.

Perhaps I did not do enough to actually take care of her, but I watched over her, that should be clear enough. Surely that must count for something. I watched for small animals, vermin, I watched for the sinister descent of dust. I made sure nothing touched her.

I fell behind in my reading, of course, and any daily list of planned activities became obsolete the minute I had completed it. That happens with children. As my mother would have said, it comes with the territory.

And I do believe that Kat appreciated this. She appeared to smile at me more often than she did at Martha. It was only later, after she was walking, that she insisted on tracking dirt into the house and handling my books without my permission, in turn dirtying them.

Sometimes I still find her handprints here, layered over some fine book cover, marring it permanently with the negative image of a dusty hand.

She was a loud child. Whether she was louder than most I have no idea, having nothing to compare her to. But certainly she was loud enough. Even at two she raced through the first floor rooms overhead, a series of overlapping thunderings so loud and obnoxious it was difficult to believe they had but a single source. And she had to touch everything she saw: antiques, good china, finely-bound books. It was as if her hands were directly connected to her eyes.

She could be so terribly, terribly loud. I cannot believe I am the only father who could not tolerate such noise. And now, I would almost miss it, if only I had the opportunity. For when the day is at its quietest I can still hear her rumblings, although more vaguely now, as if she were roaming a more distant part of the house, touching things, picking them up and looking at them. Breaking them.

I have come to realise that I count the beginnings of our real problems with Kat from about the time she turned two and started saying her first recognisable words. The process itself was endlessly fascinating, particularly for someone in love with words. Kat's almost constant wet mouthings, which I'd always taken for hunger or discomfort, suddenly gave rise to perceivable words and pairings of words. I suppose all parents are impressed by their children's first forays into language, and in this regard our family was the picture of normalcy. Every evening Martha and I would regale each other with tales of Kat's new expressions and verbal discoveries. The brevity and directness of her utterings achieved a kind of poetry we could both feel enthusiastic about. And Kat certainly inspired a certain amount of adoration as she gamboled about, chattering like an insane person.

But this preciousness soon gave way as her chatter increased in volume and persistency, and we were treated to endless repetitive monologues concerning everything she saw, ate, or felt. A trip to the bathroom might inspire a speech, the discovery of a dead moth an endless diatribe with only occasional recognisable words. I spent increasing amounts of time in my basement, and would not come even when she beat her tiny fists on my door.

No, I was not a terribly good father. But that does not mean I did not love my daughter. The only kind of love I had known before was the love of a man for a woman, or the terribly ambiguous and awkward love of a son for his parents. I did not know what to expect. The love of a man for a woman is a particular kind of tension, a repulsion and an attraction, an excitement about the "other". But the bond with Kat was something entirely different, entirely opposed. It was the sense of identity—and for me that was a unique experience, as I'd never identified with anyone before—and sameness, this feeling that Kat was yet another organ of my body, as much a part of me as my heart or lungs, but free to walk around, to speak, to think.

I must say this was not an entirely wonderful sensation. It was a strange, disembodied feeling, as if I were being haunted by myself, a perception which only increased as Kat grew older.

No one likes being reminded so frequently of himself. Not that I pretend to understand other people. But at least it was an idea, and I've had so few, I paid close attention to this one. Perhaps I thought it was an excuse for some of the things I did as her father.

Such as the times I hid in my basement when she brought her friends over. This is something young people must do, I understand, but it was all I could do to manage the commotion of my own child, much less other people's rude little brats.

Or the times she came crying to my locked door, wanting to speak to me concerning some trouble at school or dispute with a friend, or after a battle with her mother (which became more and more frequent as she grew older—sometimes I would hear them screaming overhead for hours). But I could not do it—I pretended not to hear. I did not want to take sides, had quite forgotten even how to take sides. And there was also that particular tone in her voice, that whining tone, which reminded me uncomfortably of the tone I myself used when I talked to her mother.

Terrible behaviour on my part, I know, but I could not seem to help myself. Perhaps if she had been a quieter, more peaceful child. A bit less lively.

When I did speak to her she would not listen. She does not listen to me now. She goes her own headstrong way. And fills my house with noise.

The dust in my basement rooms reached a peak during Kat's early teen years. I had some feelings that it might have something to do with the sheer quantity and volume of raw emotion in our house at the time. Or the fact that she was even more physical than ever, running in and out of rooms, up and down the stairs, slamming her schoolbooks onto the antique dining-room table, screaming at her mother, screaming at me through the floor, knowing the exact spot below which I was hiding. Creating dust in everything she did.

No matter what I tried, I could not clean up the mess.

I have read perhaps hundreds of poems about dust, a good many novels with "Dust" somewhere in the title, more than a handful of short stories. But nothing has chilled me more than true science accounts of dust mites who dwell among these bits of debris, defecating at least twenty times each day, laying a dozen or so eggs each week, eating their fill of shed human skin many times each day. Two million in an average mattress. "Skin-eating spider" is how you translate their real name, and I've seen the pictures—they look as you would imagine creatures would look who are willing to eat your skin.

Even worse is to imagine that such creatures did not exist, and each day we had to wade through rooms full of our sour dead skin.

I did not tell Kat about such things, fearing it might harm her. That seems laughable now, now that I understand the real harm I did was in not talking.

Just as I felt compelled to theorise about Kat and my relationship to her, I began to see things about the dust which I had not recognised before. Certain properties and characteristics, certain propensities. There came a time when I could no longer keep up with the fall of dust from our house's upper stories. This lack of attention was in large part due to Kat's increasing emotional outbursts and my anxiety over her safety.

Her dead skin, thousands of minute bits of it, filling the house. It was a vision I could not shake from my head.

The continuing process of her living, her dying.

Dust has accumulated here over the years to quite a remarkable depth, really. A grey halo surrounds my books, a thick and permanent shadow across their surfaces. Combined with hair and other debris, the dust has created a kind of blurred filter, a distortion through which I see everything. These layers of dust possess a kind of grain which appears to shift according to the prevailing conditions. I suspect it is due to some sort of electrical charge, perhaps emitted by the originating bodies themselves, the dust-making flesh. The dust which possesses no charge becomes merely discolouration, a permanent stain.

The police have very specific procedures for the handling of runaways these days, or so I have read in the papers. They suggest that you put the child's clothing in a box and fill it with sand, so that she cannot return for a quick change of clothes. The sand also preserves DNA evidence if a body, or a murderer, must be identified. It is the times people are living in, I suppose. I am pleased not to be a part of that. I have not been a part of any of that since Kat disappeared and Martha died in the car accident—she was quite depressed, I know, but I refuse to imagine it as suicide. Bad enough that I could not make myself touch her during those times when the police came and asked their questions, and the neighbours helped her search and wondered aloud why I stayed in my basement and would not join them.

I loved my wife, despite my inattention.

Eventually I retired from my job—I was an editor in the department by then and did no real work anymore. With Martha's insurance I did not need to work—there was plenty to cover delivered food and regular mail order book purchases. Sometimes I am able to pile enough new books over the old to disguise the deteriorating effects of the dust.

I love my Kat as well, and I refuse to imagine her dead. Even though it has been twenty years with no further word. Some might say I am a man of little imagination.

So much dust. So much dust that I cough when I turn the pages. And choke up when I read aloud, eager for the sound of a voice in the room. But the dust is slowly denying me even that. I can feel the tears changing to mud tracks on my cheeks. The dust gets in my eyes and clogs my throat. For there is no sadness in me—I cannot bring myself to imagine sadness.

Kat would be in her thirties now. So all these small handprints appearing on the surface of book after book could not possibly be hers.

And these small handprints on the windows, and on the walls and ceilings. Upon closer examination I have discovered that these prints were not caused by the absence of dust, the moisture and pressure of the hand removing dust to make these prints. No, these prints are made of dust, the imprints of dust hands. Somehow children have got inside with their dirty little hands.

But that is fine, that is a thing which can be accepted. Everyone knows how much I have always loved children, everyone in town knows this. The least they could do is speak to me, chatter away through their meaningless little tales. It does not matter. I will not be able to understand a thing they say.

Kat, you must listen to me. Whatever you wish to say to me, I will not understand your words. It just is not in me.

Some might say I am a man of little imagination. Some might say I have haunted my life rather than lived it. But I simply enjoy a quiet place in which to sit and read, to watch the slow fall of dust and the many shapes it reveals.

Inside William James

illiam James? Time to wake up, honey.

He did not really believe it was his mother speaking to him. He knew what people said about him, but he had more sense than that. He didn't always remember things right, but he still had all his marbles. He smiled because that was a joke. He had a big cloth bag full of marbles under his bed that he traded with, always fair about it but still trying to get the better deal. If anybody needed proof he was no dummy, all they had to do was watch the way he traded those marbles.

Out in the big world nobody paid attention to such things as marbles and trades and William James. Out in the big world folks had bigger fish to fry, and they weren't sharing those fish with the likes of William James. The younger kids were the only ones cared about trading marbles with old William James. The only ones. He wouldn't cheat the younger kids. Not that he'd ever cheated anybody, but even if he felt he had to cheat somebody for something real important—to save the world maybe, big world and little world and all the places people and fishes lived—he still wouldn't cheat one of those little kids, kids what had to be protected from the bad traders in the world.

But he'd still try to get himself the better deal because that was what trading was all about. Not too better, not to take the other people's marbles he didn't deserve, especially not the little kidses.

You've been sleeping too long, William James.

But William James knew there was no such thing as sleeping too long. Bed was a good place, maybe the best place, and nobody had the right to ask you to leave it unless they were your mother.

That wasn't his mother's voice but he pretended it might be. That didn't make him a little kid, did it? But it sure made him sad. Sure, he got to talk to his mother some way or other most every day, but it wasn't the same since she was dead. She got tired easy and didn't want to talk too much. Being dead, William James decided, took a lot out of you.

William James . . .

His eyes opened up like butterflies, a few flying away at a time. He couldn't stop them—you couldn't catch every butterfly that came around. They were like nervous people who didn't know how to behave, so they did what they worried on, and didn't think about if it was wrong or not.

The woman had a big face, not nervous at all, and not like his mother's face.

"Hey, Nurse Bossy," he said to the face.

"Hey, William James. Time for breakfast." She smiled. Nurse Bossy was what he called her, but it was kind of a joke. She told him what to do, all right, and he didn't much like that, but she could be pretty nice about it, saying things that sometimes made him smile. And he had known her as long as he'd been here. He loved her.

"Do I have to, Nurse Bossy?"

"You have to eat, child! If you don't eat you die."

William James nodded. He couldn't argue with that, but he didn't like her talking about things he didn't like thinking about. He didn't want to talk anymore.

She stood by while he got dressed, just in case he made a mistake. But he almost never did. He was the last one to the breakfast table but that usually happened no matter how fast he went.

He did what he always did when he first sat down: looked around to see if there was anybody he didn't know. Sometimes there would be somebody new and he'd have to get up and go shake their hand just because that's the kind of person he was. Or maybe wanted to be. He couldn't remember. The nurses always said it was "a nice gesture", but sometimes they had to calm a new person down when William James went over and grabbed their hand like that.

He didn't think there was anybody new just then so he started to dig into his eggs and sausage—sometimes he made the eggs smile and stuck the sausage in like a big C-gar, but when he was really hungry time was a wasting and the food was for eating not for making faces up at you.

And then he saw the new face.

The new face came right out of the big freezer door like he'd been on skiing vacation and sat down at the next table across from William James and stared at William like he was one of those fancy fruit cups they had for breakfast on extra special occasions when lots of visitors came.

William James didn't know exactly who it was, but he sure knew what it was he'd seen that kind so many times before. The face all grey and the hair burned off, big patches on the skin dark like wet leaves been run over by a car a hundred hundred times. He didn't like this kind of new at all, so he tried to look down at his breakfast, follow the stripes in the bacon back and forth and around where it curled into the burned part. He tried to pretend the new one in the eating room was a lamp with the bulb burned out, just waiting to be taken out to the trash.

Didn't work.

After a while he looked back up at the new one, stared it right in the ugly, and stuck his tongue out.

The new one stuck his own tongue right back at him, and it was like a bone spoon full of black ashes and it made William James shake all over, like he was looking into a bad dream mirror. At himself.

William James got out of the chair and walked right over to the new one, spilling a few of the other people who lived there out onto the floor, where they whimpered or bawled or threw up, depending on what they were best at that day. "You ain't me!" he yelled at the bad ash face. "But give here," he said, throwing his arm right up to the ugly burnt nose, "Shake!"

Bad Ash Face just stared, and William James could see then that even the man's eyeballs were burned. That made him swallow some, but he still held his hand steady as he could. "Go on, take it! It's a nice gesture."

And when the Ash Face wouldn't, William James tried to grab the new one's hand and make him shake hands. And felt his own hand tingle, like a little bit of the skin on his fingers was peeling back, and then his hand went through all that ash and skin and came out the other side.

William James felt other hands then, on his back and shoulders, a couple on his sides, pulling him back and down to the floor. He tried to fight his way free, swinging and punching people he didn't really want to hurt, but didn't feel he could choose not to, either.

"William James, what's come over you?" That was Nurse Bossy—Nurse Betty—right behind him and he made himself not hurt her.

"Tell me he ain't me!" he cried, pulling his arm loose enough to point. "And tell him that, too."

But the Ugly Ash Face was already mostly gone. Just a smear of sooty skin here and there like something on a dirty old window. And then that little bit cleaned off, and there was nothing.

Nurse Betty was terribly sorry but she had to ask him to stay in his room that night.He was real sorry too, for scaring everybody the way he did. There wasn't a mirror in the room, but the dresser was pretty shiny, and if he put the lamp on it just right he could see his reflection pretty good.

He had some scars all right, but nothing like that Ugly Ash Face. His were small and smooth and here and there, like somebody had taken a giant eraser to his face and tried to rub out the lines.

William James. William James? Time to get up now—haven't you slept long enough?

William James didn't know how to answer a question like that; he just kept his eyes shut so he could think about it for a while. Inside William James things were all stirred up. People were moving in and out of houses and there were boxes everywhere, going on trucks and being carried inside, shoved around on the floor and stacked in the backs of closets. The cars on the street were old and broken down, so everywhere people were walking. Then the sky got bright enough to turn the houses orange, and everywhere inside William James people were walking with their heads on fire, even the younger kids, and they didn't even know it, walking around like giant burning matches.

"Hey, Nurse Bossy," he said, opening his eyes.

"Time for breakfast, William James. Do you feel well enough to come down to the dining room, or do you think it best that you stay in your room a while longer?"

William James closed his eyes to think. That was the longest question anyone had asked him in a very long time. He sat down in the middle of the street to think about it. He didn't worry about any cars coming and running him over because none of the cars were running.

The sun was falling down out of the sky a few blocks away. A couple of houses caught fire and nearby a car or two exploded. The sirens came but they forgot their fire engines and all the firemen that usually rode on the fire engines' backs. So the sirens just stood out in the street and screamed at the burning houses. By the time they were done screaming the sun had finished its burning and the sky was black. The street lights came on but the sky was still like shiny coal with fireflies resting here and resting there, burning themselves on and burning themselves off.

People were walking through the yards and walking through the streets, all of them going someplace where the light was the brightest. So William James got up to follow, thinking that whenever a lot of people go to one place there's always food, and William James was hungry enough to eat anything, even if it wasn't cooked right, even if it was burnt.

But then he saw Ugly Ash Face, who smiled at him and waved, then came over and tried to shake William James's hand. But the worst thing was that Ugly Ash Face wasn't so ugly right then, and William James recognized him as a neighbour who used to live down the street from him.

William James tried to turn around then, but there were so many people pushing their way into that house he couldn't turn against them. Before he knew it he was inside, and practically everybody was making a nice gesture, shaking his hand and telling him what a lucky young man he was.

And there was his mother, all shiny like a Bluebird in her favourite party dress. She had little brownies with red hearts on them she was handing out, and everybody was saying how yummy yummy yummy they were, but when she handed one to William James he just couldn't eat it. He couldn't bite into one of those bright red hearts.

Don't get him too fat before the wedding, Maria! the man on William's right said, taking a brownie in his burning hand, the chocolate melting across his fingers, the red icing dripping to the floor. *Then his pretty bride won't want him!* The man laughed, the inside of his mouth vanishing into flame, the fire burning up through the skull and escaping where the nose used to be.

William James ran out of the room, up the stairs to where he knew his room, his bed must be. He jerked open his bedroom door and the first thing he saw were his marbles scattered across the floor. He hadn't thought about his marbles in years, he hadn't played with them since he was a little fellow, but he'd kept them special in a fancy cloth bag his mother had made for him, tucked up under the bed against the wall.

Now they were scattered everywhere, eyes and jewels and little round jellyfish, on the floor with the light dying inside them.

And on the bed lay his fiancée Elise, her pretty gown in disarray, still holding on to his brother Carlos, crying and telling William James not to be angry with her, that she had been feeling a little sick and Carlos was just helping her, after all they would be family soon, but still holding on to Carlos as if she didn't know what else to do.

But William James could no longer look at Elise and his brother, so his eyes found something else to look at: the marbles everywhere, and the dying light flickering inside them, and his eyes seeking the source of that flicker found the candles he'd bought placed in every corner of the room, the candles he had told his brother about, all their different smells like being inside a burning flower shop, the candles he'd planned to load into his car for his wedding night, when he would put them around their marriage bed, hundreds of flames and smells for his beloved Elise.

He gazed at his brother Carlos, who stared back with those not-sorry eyes. Who was not stupid. Who knew he would be caught like this, in his brother's bed, with his brother's candles, his brother's fiancée. It was only Elise who might not have fully understood, Elise who had been stupid, but never as stupid as William James himself.

William James could feel the anger charging his muscles like electricity; his fists curled on their own, tight enough to cause him pain. He looked away from Carlos and Elise, determined that he would not step toward them, and looked at the candles instead, the ones he'd picked and bought from every place he knew that sold candles, their combined scents so thick and heavy now they smelled like layers of garbage. He swung a forearm into the dozen or so on his desk, and those in turn toppled dozens more. Unable to stop himself, even after his shirt caught fire, he waded swinging into the tiers of candles, dancing through the flames, his legs kicking into heat and his lungs ragged and rough with smoke. Now and then he felt their hands on him trying to stop him, but they gave up right away, and he was dancing alone. In some distant place inside him William James could hear the last of their singing: his mother, the rest of his family, friends and neighbours, Elise.

William James . . . William James . . .

Nurse Betty showed him a worried person's face, and others were there with angry faces and faces that didn't care either way. They helped him up and sat him in a chair, and one of the doctors checked him over and after he said what he had to say everybody but Nurse Betty left him there.

"You'll be okay for breakfast, won't you, William James?"

William James nodded. "No trouble," he said, and busied himself getting dressed with Nurse Betty watching him. For a little bit he was confused with his socks until Nurse Betty took them away and got them started for him. He felt embarrassed, but grateful to her just the same.

Breakfast was almost over by the time he got to the dining room, but they fed him anyway. Most of the other residents had left—he could hear one of them crying out in the hallway and figured it must be Jimmy.

He looked around at all the new faces. Some of them he had seen once or twice the past few months, but others were new new, and had never been here before. Some of them looked like women from the old neighbourhood. Some of them looked like men he'd known all his life. Ashen hair and blasted skin, now they all looked his kin. Some of them nodded his way, and then looked back down at their hands. They smelled like smoke and garbage. They were his mother's friends, and all had come to his party.

William . . . William James . . .

His mother's breath was like a warm candle. It tickled the inside of his throat. William James opened his mouth and waited for his mother to come out.

Back Among the Shy Trees

He came back to the county late at night, a mistake, having forgotten how dark it could be with light poles and house lights so few and far between. But he'd had no choice given how far away he'd travelled to build a new life, and the limited time off he'd begged from his job, and having next to no money for a motel.

At least in the dark there had been little change. His headlights picked their way through poorly paved roads winding through the rolling countryside. The woods made a constant impending presence across the fields, but with occasional surprising surges when it appeared to run up to the very windows of the car.

For most of the trip, however, the forest here was a comfortable distance away, its unbroken mass jewelled intermittently with the bright reflected gaze of spying animals. What sparked such curiosity Tyler had never understood—how many cars had they seen from their vantage points along the road? He would have thought they'd be fed up with the human race by now, turned their backs on the annoying neighbours. Or perhaps it was the motor vehicles they considered their true visitors on the road, the human beings merely the noisome meals the vehicles had eaten.

A short distance from that house he'd grown up in and long ago escaped, he passed through the small town he barely remembered, so quickly it but vaguely registered:

dark storefronts on both sides of the narrow street, a crumbling raised sidewalk, the only illumination the blinking yellow caution light like a defective eye at the top of the hill. By chance he caught a glimpse of something reflected deep in the last shop window he passed—a late burning light or another pair of eyes.

Then that compact village was gone again, hardly worth a thought. Immediately on its outskirts the woods drew near again, as if eager for some homecoming embrace. Their texture was ragged, almost furry, as if the long line of trees had become this great reclining, sleeping beast.

The house that had once so forcefully contained him and his sister was planted stubbornly into a gentle hill a few turns past. Its basement was deeper than most, his father said, in order to resist the high winds passing through this part of the valley. Here the shy trees had receded almost entirely, back to provide a dark fringe to the horizon, in fact much farther back than he recalled. All through his childhood the neighbouring trees had disappeared, as if being cleared for farms or housing which never materialised. And as the trees disappeared, the winds, increasingly unobstructed, battered the house until every joint howled; but his dead forebears had built it strong—it still held its grip on the land, like some steel-clawed animal dumb in its intensity.

But there had always been that one spindly and barren apple tree by the front walk, improbably small—he remembered it being there most of his life—but it hadn't grown at all, just as his family hadn't increased. He and his sister had each determined not to have kids of their own. But that singular tree was large enough to emphasise the barrenness of the yard—their parents had had an unhindered view for miles from any window—making it clear that surreptitious escape or assault would always be an improbable feat.

So Tyler slammed the car door thinking it made no difference, even though he hated the gunshot sound it made in the still air. He might as well arrive boldly when discretion was not an option. The lights inside the house remained dark. No one at home, of course.

The house was rough-made, wooden, and not all the clapboard siding was of the same width, length, or style. It had been pieced together by generations of his family who cared very little for consistency or grace, only that it held, and that what was inside stayed. And certainly this ancient disaster of a house had stood while others in the county had failed, in wind, in lightning, or from a lack of passion. His people had cared nothing about each other, and even less for those outside, but they had passion for where they stood and where they slept. Kindness might have made others sleep better, but not them. His people fed on anger—they grew old and strong on the wellsprings of their hatred.

Since Tyler had left here he'd met people who at least pretended to know every aspect of their childhoods, able to recount in detail some long afternoon spent when they were twelve years old almost as if it had happened yesterday. He didn't know what to make of these accounts. For him childhood had always been this frantic blur, with only a few images resolving themselves, and those with little emotion attached. He suspected people made too much of their histories.

The key his sister had mailed him slipped loosely into the lock, as if too small to open up something so large, but it turned, and there was a distant sound as something changed. The door clicked, and then fell open, as if released to gravity. He stepped inside clutching a large flashlight. There would be no lights, no power after all this time.

A thick layer of grey dust fed silently on his parents' things, which had been reduced to indistinct shapes beneath the filth. The nastiness wasn't unexpected, but the nerves inside the roots of several of his teeth suddenly came alive. His mother had gone into the hospital and never returned, dying years later in some anonymous facility. A week into her hospitalisation, his father had disappeared. People who did not know his father said he'd just walked away from his life. Tyler suspected the opposite: he'd finally found the life waiting for him. In any case, people who abdicate so abruptly rarely tidy up. No one had touched the insides of this place since then.

Tyler had been long gone by that point, and had received all this information second hand. His sister had lived it, and immediately after had been spirited away to a succession of distant and indifferent relatives. He thought he should feel badly about that, and for years had played with a kind of theoretical guilt, but it had never stuck. And his sister had always been too cold to resent it. In that way both had been very much their parents' children.

At their mother's funeral Tyler and his sister had exchanged a scatter of brief observations regarding the weather, the position of the sun, the uncharacteristic lack of wind. Their mother was buried on land they owned, in a lot where her people had always been interred, at some distance from the house but within its watch.

Then Carol had looked at him. "Have you seen him?"

"Who?" She would not take the bait. Finally he had replied, "No."

"He's probably dead then," she said, and it might have been the most hopeful sentence he'd ever heard pass her lips.

But again he replied, "No."

One of the few things Tyler did remember about his childhood was the tree house they'd built when he was ten in the nearest edge of the woods. The trees had been much closer back then, only a grass field away. Collaborating on a project had surprised both of them. Tyler couldn't remember who had suggested it, but he supposed it was like two people in a burning house—they were both drawn independently to the open door. The platform high in the trees gave them a clear view of the back of the house in case their father came to look for them. Tyler would wonder later why their father had ever allowed them to build such a thing, but then realised the man could have gone up after them at any time. That feeling of freedom and safe distance had been illusory.

Tyler had feared their father—they both had—but wasn't quite sure why, and they had never discussed it. He'd rarely punished them, and shouting was rarer still. But he had a way of looking at you with eyes of such chilly indifference you were never really sure if he was seeing you at all—you simply knew that avoiding prolonged exposure was best.

When Tyler fell out of the tree house that summer and broke his leg, Carol had returned calmly to the house to share this information with their parents. Their father had suggested she put Tyler in her Red Flyer wagon and instructed their mother to help her drag him to the road to flag down a passing neighbour. He hadn't bothered to put down his paper or get up from his chair.

The tree house had burned several nights later along with a significant portion of the woods. When the county sheriff questioned the family no one had claimed credit.

The house had a slightly oily smell, an animal stink, although it wasn't immediately evident why. Tyler was averse to touching any of the dust-encrusted things, and possessed little natural curiosity, but felt some urgency about completing the planned task. He had no more love for his current job than for any other, but he needed the money for the bills it paid. What his task here was, he'd never been quite sure. The envelope containing the key from his sister also contained a note explaining that someone wanted to buy the place for development, and reminding him that although she had the papers and been the last to leave, the property legally had been theirs to share. "Brother," she wrote, and it struck him how this was the most intimately she'd addressed him in years, "I will not go back into that house. If there is anything of value it is yours to take." Needless to say there was no generosity in her statement, but he never passed up an opportunity for money, or things to sell. He did not know how to feel, exactly, when she wrote further that the new owners would tear the house down. But his first thought had been *of course*, as if there could be no other outcome. Then he'd thought, *but I wonder if that's possible?*

He pulled a handkerchief from his pocket, and with the first swipe at the mass of dust-encased objects on the dining room table it came away black and furry. He looked for antiques or at least things finely made, and, finding none, went on.

Initially he had no memory of any of the things he found. Cups and saucers, bowls, silverware—he had no recollection of using any of them. He had a vague image in his head of numerous chalky figurines his mother had displayed on various shelves and tables around the house. He found a few of these, perhaps, but their features were so worn, the dust having adhered to details in what seemed a permanent bond, he couldn't be sure what they were intended to represent. Gnomes, perhaps, or cherubs, or just lumps of nothing whose specifics you were supposed to imagine.

A hairbrush with a rose painted on the back did seem somewhat familiar—he thought he remembered his mother sitting in front of a mirror, brushing her hair with it. There was hair still snagged on the bristles, coated and lengthened with threads of grey dust, which if he followed would take him someplace he did not want to be. Old cosmetic bottles, open and unopened, lay about the tables and shelves, rolling underfoot, most of their labels unreadable.

Pieces of toys, nothing complete, as if they'd been cannibalised for some other purpose. Piles of magazine clippings offering glimpses of a normal life. Many had stuck together, or were badly stained by organic matter. But still nothing Tyler remembered touching, holding.

Photographs in cheap, even handmade frames, propped up on surfaces, or hanging askew on the walls. One of them might have been his father—at least the scowl looked accurate. And a picture of his sister, turned much older (like she was now?) which must in fact be their mother. He didn't recognise any of the people in the other pictures—they might have been random purchases from a thrift store for all he knew—but he developed a theory that the people who were more formally dressed had been part of his mother's family, with their ties and suits and fancy, old-fashioned hats, their smiling faces.

The other photographs he arbitrarily assigned to his father's side of the family. The faces were out-of-focus, sometimes reduced to smudges of a stormy grey. Even in the ones of better focus, the subjects had turned away from the camera, shielded their eyes, or blocked the photographer's intrusion with their hands. Their clothes were worn, shapeless, and monochromatic. In one or two the faces had been further obscured by some sharp object that had scratched the emulsion away.

Tyler had met some members of his mother's family when he was small, he believed, but never any of his father's relatives. Once he had asked his mother (he never asked his father anything) if his father's people lived too far away to visit. She'd replied with some agitation, "Oh, they are quite close," but then she'd refused to explain any more.

A few hours before dawn, Tyler was on his way to bed—a cot set up in his old bedroom (he wasn't about to lie on any of *this* bedding)—when he heard a scratching noise at the front door. He considered ignoring it, but when the scratching persisted he unlatched the door and jerked it open. A large grey dog trotted in, snarling, swinging its head back and forth, and sniffing everything it passed. Reaching the far wall it stopped and turned around, staring at Tyler, its lips rippling along the line of exposed teeth. Tyler thought it was some kind of hound.

The dog continued to snarl, its legs tensing as it edged forward. Tyler stared at it, feeling annoyed, but not much else. Maybe the dog had been in this house before; maybe the dog had as much right to be here as he had. He wasn't sure why he wasn't frightened, perhaps it was unfamiliarity—he'd never had a dog or any other pet—had never even considered it. Or perhaps he was too tired for fright. "Shut up or leave," he told the dog. The dog shut up, and Tyler allowed it to lead him into the bedroom, where it stretched out on the floor in front of the cot.

He woke up to the sound of a gentle rain on the roof and house walls. It must have been close to dawn—a cold, dark blue glow illuminated the rectangles of window. He saw the dog standing by the closest window, staring outside. Tyler joined it.

There had been no rain. Dead insects—moths, grasshoppers, a variety of beetles—covered the lawn and the roof and hood of his car. More fell from the sky, making a soft patter as they struck the house, the car, the insect bodies that had already fallen. The dog panted loudly beside him, its eyes shifting, watching as each new corpse hit.

Then the dog pulled back a few steps from the window, a slight edge of growl coming back into its throat. Tyler watched as the horizon filled with ragged shadow, then flowed rapidly toward him, and trees spilled over his lawn, the shiny eyes among them multiplying, growing brighter as they fed.

Tyler peeled himself off his cot the next morning, not having remembered going back to bed. In the grimy yellow light the house looked even worse—the walls smeared with dirt, everything jumbled, coated, crumbling, the light catching the ebb and flow of airborne dust as it moved through the rooms, and for the first time he could really see the cobwebs, the dust webs, that filigreed everything, that connected it all into a pattern of disuse and neglect. The dog—*yes, there had been a dog!*—stood by the front window looking out, so transfixed it didn't even bother turning around when Tyler came into the front room. The dog seemed somewhat smaller than it had the night before.

Then he remembered the dream—sure it had been a dream even though it certainly didn't feel like it—but he'd awakened on the cot so it must have been a dream. If it had really happened he would have stayed by the window, transfixed, like that changeable dog.

He stood by the dog, which still ignored him. There was nothing on the dry and uncared-for front lawn except a sloppy beard of weeds. The shy trees were safely back in the horizon. There was a single small grasshopper wrapped in webbing on the windowsill waiting to be eaten, but no others. Nothing unusual. His car looked as worn and dusty as everything else parked up onto the edge of the yard, but nothing unusual about that either. The best thing for him would be to finish going through these old forgotten things—at least that would satisfy his sister's demands—then leave the county and return to his life.

After a couple of hours it became pretty clear that there was very little here he'd be taking home to sell. He'd started a box and so far had put some silver candlesticks in there, a couple of fancy ladles, and a few small glass objects that might be antique but probably weren't, but with nothing better turning up he'd at least take them back for appraisal.

The dog was nosing aggressively through a box in what he figured must have been his sister's old bedroom. There was no bed in there, however, or dresser, or even anything vaguely "girl-like". But he still had a pretty clear memory that that was where it had been—certainly he hadn't found anything identifiably hers anywhere else. What had she slept on all those years? There was no way to know— he'd never be able to ask her.

He checked out the box the dog had been messing with and found two small photos of himself with his sister. He had no pictures of her, and was unlikely to have any in the future, so he'd take them, even though he had no particular desire to show them in his house. It was just that if you had a sister, people expected you to have a picture of her, that was all.

There were also one or two pictures of his parents together—his mother smiling stupidly, his father looking away—which he would leave behind. And there were a lot more photographs like the framed ones on the walls— people in formal wear, grinning awkwardly, but many more of unidentifiable, smeared humanity, turned away, unfocused, or deliberately marred. His father's people, destined for anonymity.

Eventually it occurred to him that so far he'd found no newspapers, or books, not even a phone book. Had they had a phone? He had no memory of either of his parents talking on a phone, or of a phone ringing. He wasn't a serious reader himself, and owned no books, but had always read the newspaper religiously, front to back. It explained the world.

About midday Tyler found the dog wandering around somewhat frantically, whimpering, sticking its head muzzle-deep into every box, pot, bag, or container. Then he realised the nagging ache he'd been feeling was hunger, and he'd brought no food along.

He grabbed his jacket off the front door knob and jerked open the door. The dog bounded to his side. Tyler looked down at it, but couldn't quite bring himself to look into its eyes. He considered, and found himself speaking to the floor, shy about the interaction. "I won't be taking you into town, but I'll bring you back some food. You stay here and, just *stay*. Guard the place, whatever."

As he walked to his car he saw pine needles on the ground. He looked around—they were all over, the yard was covered in them. At least he didn't see any bugs. But once he got into his car he could see two or three insects lying on top of the windshield wipers. One was on its back, stiff legs frozen while scratching at the faraway sky. He started the car and shot fluid onto the windshield, wiped them away.

He drove back into the small town he'd passed through the night before. Winton. It rang no bells, but he was pretty sure he'd been here several times as a child. How could he not have—wasn't it the closest town to their house? For years they were home-schooled by their mother, although he could not now imagine that silly woman managing such a chore. But she must have done well enough—when he did read, he understood what he read. He didn't always understand what they were talking about on television, but then most subjects did not interest him. They had nothing to do with him or his life. So he watched very little TV—he didn't even own a set. Sometimes they'd have one on in a restaurant or at the barber shop. It annoyed him.

He was pretty sure he'd gone to some sort of elementary school for a year or two in this town or some other. He remembered being in a classroom with other children but not really being there. His mind was always somewhere else, they'd said. For his senior year he'd gone to the public school—his mother stopped teaching them at home for some reason. He wasn't aware of what his sister had done. Maybe she'd stopped attending at all by that point. He remembered he'd had a long bus ride, and hadn't enjoyed the school very much—he'd kept to himself, and didn't like to talk. They'd given him a diploma, however, and then he'd left the county forever. Until now.

He seemed to be remembering more and more the longer he was here. He didn't like it; it wasn't useful to him. He had to finish the job and leave.

Today he could see that there were a dozen or so people walking around in the town. But still, many of the stores were dark. He walked into the one with the Grocery sign.

There were several people inside, but he fought the urge to leave. The long fluorescent bulbs overhead made the single room almost painfully bright. He took a cart and walked slowly down the aisles. He did not recognise most of the brands, and many of the products themselves, but he was able to load his cart with soups, bread, and peanut butter. He searched for, and found, a knife for the peanut butter, not wanting to use any of the silverware from the house. Then he remembered there was no power to cook with, so he put the soups back.

Normally, at home in his present life, he bought the exact same things from the store every week. Here he had no idea what to buy.

He stood in front of the shelves of dog food, studying them. He had no idea if this was an old dog or a young dog, or if it needed "weight control" or some special diet. Was it a "large breed" dog? He didn't know. He found a dog food with just a brand name and "Dog Food" on the bag. He got the largest bag and put that one into his cart, figuring he would leave it with the dog when he left the county again.

There was a fellow in front of him at the checkout counter buying all sweet things—candies and cookies. Tyler looked away, and then didn't know where to look. Finally his gaze rested on the ceiling. When he came up to the cash register the elderly clerk stared at him an uncomfortable period of time then said, "You're one of the Colliers, ain't you?"

Tyler was embarrassed, and angry that he was embarrassed. "Yes," he said softly.

"Back in town to visit your dad?"

Was the man playing with him? But he didn't want to ask any questions that might extend the conversation. "I—haven't seen him," he said, watching the man take his money and bag his groceries.

"Never got along with my dad, neither," the man said, sighing. "I see your dad around town sometimes, a couple of times a week, I reckon, but he don't come in here and we never speak. Don't know where he's getting his groceries, then."

"Oh." Tyler tried to keep his face still.

"But you still give him my regards, you hear?" The man handed Tyler the groceries. Tyler nodded wordlessly and left.

He and the dog sat together consuming their respective meals. Tyler put the large bag of dog food down and just made a hole in the middle of it. He regretted the choice at once. The dog attacked the bag with such ferocity he was eating both dog nuggets and paper, and very quickly had chewed through the bag and all the way to the debris-covered floor, coming up with bits of dusty paper and trash in the corners of its broad jaw.

Tyler looked away and would not look at the animal again until the dog had calmed down. He made sandwich after sandwich of peanut butter and spongy bread, devouring them to the accompaniment of the growling, whimpering sounds of the dog's eating. He stopped only when he felt stomach acid beginning to lap at the bottom of his throat.

As much as he didn't want to drive the county roads at night again he would have loved to leave that evening. There was nothing more here of value, certainly nothing he'd like to carry back in the car with him. He never should have come, and found it difficult not to be furious with his sister for sending the key with the letter that dragged him back here.

But although the light was rapidly escaping this long day he felt that for the sake of completeness he needed to explore the basement. Of course there would be nothing of value there but he could write his sister back and tell her he'd searched all parts of the house including the basement, even though he didn't want to go there. He didn't care about her opinion but he still wanted it on the record.

He loaded fresh batteries into the flashlight and with much effort jerked open the swollen basement door in the kitchen. It scraped the old linoleum with a horrendous sound, cracking off several large pieces of flooring. The dog kept its distance on the other side of the kitchen. Tyler glanced at the animal before going down the stairs, the dog unmoving, whimpering softly as he descended. He didn't close the door.

The staircase was surprisingly steep, hugging first a stone, and then a bare dirt wall as it descended deeper underground. It was rickety and poorly made, added to over the years with a variety of plywood and sheet metal, reinforced with brackets from autos, appliances, and other inexplicable jerry-rigging. He wondered how many different hands had added to its construction over the decades.

He could hear the dog howling at the kitchen door, as if it wanted him to come back, as if it hadn't wanted him to go down in the first place. Had anyone in his life before cared that much what he did? He didn't think so. To his surprise, he realised then he'd be taking the dog home with him.

The further he stepped down, the more intense an oily, animal smell became, worse than what he had first smelled. He came to places where sections of the dirt walls had been hollowed out into small chambers, their roofs supported with a puzzle of old beams, planks, and posts. Littered inside were a jumble of stained rags and decaying cardboard that stank of meat, decay, and the outhouse. When he pointed his flashlight on the back walls, rats scurried away into tunnel openings large enough for a dog, or a small man. Perhaps the house wouldn't be so hard to demolish after all, if the new developer even needed to. All he really had to do was blow out a bit more dirt and the house would fall whole into the resulting pit. He remembered his father referring to the family home as a tooth anchored deep into the ground. But clearly its roots were rotten.

Tyler came to a wooden platform filling the space. He flashed his light around and saw that it was full of boxes, and near one corner was a large square hole. He stepped over a few boxes and pointed his beam there—more steps leading further down, and his flashlight couldn't find the end of them. He went over to the boxes and started going through them. In several there were more photographs similar to what he had seen before, a few with those people trying to look their best in their fanciest clothes, those earnest, nervous, desperate-looking smiles. But many more were of the marred, smeared, out-of-focus variety; some included children, a boy and a girl, but he couldn't identify who they were.

In another box he found white shirts, ties, a few nice hats, old-fashioned trousers like the ones worn in some of those earnest-looking photographs. And in another box were school papers, drawings, some with his name in crude crayon, others bearing Carol's name. He could not remember any of these drawings—they'd been made so long ago, in a different life.

In his drawings the faces were blurred—tiny fingers had pushed and smeared the lines and colours, entire heads turned into blobs of unreadable features. He thought to put one of the drawings in his pocket to take away from here, and then thought better of it.

He shone the light into the dark rectangular gap in the platform with the steps that led down and down into an even darker space. Some hazy, smeared memory nagged at him as he placed his feet and started down. Once or twice he thought he had caught up to that teasing memory, and brought it up into the light, but each time it eluded him.

After several steps he found the two cages nested into spaces hollowed out of the black earthen wall. He probed them gingerly with the light beam, as if the flashlight were somehow reluctant to see. The cages smelled foul, littered with rotting clothing—small jeans, little dresses scattered in the sour-smelling straw bedding. He reached out and grabbed the cage on the left, rattled it, rattled it, trying to remember, and remembered that metal rattle sound, and the feel of the straw on his back and legs, and the absolute dark, and the mewling sound from the other cage.

On his frantic, violent rush back up the stairs, the light swung across the walls, the shaky wooden structure, and the collapsing boxes as he panted and swallowed his despair. He grabbed some of the fancy clothes and continued up, stripping off his shirt as he continued up, wrapping the tie tight around his neck as he continued up toward the kitchen.

He came out of the basement, hearing that slow rain on the roof again, and stumbled through the house fixing his tie, and went to the front window where the dog was already standing, watching what was happening outside.

Hundreds of small birds fell out of the sky, making a soft pattering on the roof, on the bodies of their kin, making a metallic, rain-like ping as they bounced off his car.

And the trees were coming out of their retreat, flowing out from the horizon, flooding over the lawn, rushing the house.

He turned around with his flashlight, found himself in a nearby mirror, tucked in his shirt, rearranged his tie, tried to make himself presentable. It was hopeless, hopeless, for there was nothing presentable about him. But he made himself believe he resembled his mother's side of the family more and more each day.

The eyes were already at the window, looking in. The dog growled, lay on his belly and growled some more. One shadowed face came closer than the others, the outline of the head losing resolution around the edges as if drawn with a bearded, fuzzy line. Tyler thought about the dog, wondered if his father might take the dog instead, wondered what would happen if he told his father where his sister lived, wondered so many things, and knew he could not make the trade. The eyes in the dark outline of head blinked brightly, and Tyler looked back into the dim imperfect mirror, at his features dissolving, his head a growing smear, and now convinced whose side of the family he resembled more, Tyler reluctantly opened the door.

Seeing the Woods

She bought the cabin on the small plot when her eyesight began to fail. Her plan was that within the small but varied landscape of the property she might learn every tree, every large stone, each bush and clump of flowers, the places where the land dipped, where wrinkles and folds occurred, and where she might sit for an unobstructed face full of breeze. Then, as the light began to dim on the world outside her head, she might transfer those details to the lands inside.

Her daughters did not approve of the plan. Ellen, the older and more practical, had always been just shy of a bully. "You can't do that, Mother! You need to be here so that once you're blind we can take care of you. What if you went outside that cabin and couldn't find your way back? Remember those articles I brought you last winter about elderly people dying of exposure? That could be you!"

Susan sat quietly through this speech kneading her hands. And even though Liz did not particularly desire the input of either daughter, old habits of mothering always kicked in where her shy child was concerned. "Susan, sweetheart, I'm sure you have some good ideas," she said encouragingly. "What's your opinion about all this?"

Susan sniffed and gazed at her mother. The lines of her face suddenly went soft and blurred so that Liz felt as if she were looking at an old, poorly-taken photograph of someone she used to know but had not seen in years.

"This just seems unnecessary." Susan might have been crying, but she often sounded that way. "You don't know you're actually going to be blind—this might be as bad as it gets. Don't you want to be near us, as long as possible?"

Liz attempted to assuage her daughters' feelings as much as possible, but of course she bought the cabin eventually, moving in shortly thereafter.

The process of learning her new world was—once she cleared her head enough to see it—remarkably simple, really. It was mostly just a matter of being bold enough to slow down.

The cabin's basic layout presented no challenge: a main room with fireplace and kitchen area, two rooms and a bath through doors on the western side. The detail and complication she would need to keep an old mind stimulated to the end all lay outside.

Each morning she stepped carefully onto the tiny porch and felt her way down the three steps to the ground. Given her arthritis and diminished eyesight she already had to take it slow, but she deliberately cut her natural pace by half or more to encourage the leisurely intake of detail. Someday soon she would need to try to manoeuvre through her limited holdings as quickly as her capabilities permitted, simply to experience that kind of exhilaration and excitement generated when the pulse quickens and the breathing lags, an understanding she could file away until later when infirmity would not permit such exertion. But for now her priority was to discover the rhythm which would maximise her knowledge of her surroundings.

So each day she crept around her property, counting steps, closing her eyes to see if she could still divine directions, touching everything with her hands, gauging slope and hardness and texture through her thin-soled shoes. With only minimal study she was quickly able to identify the few varieties of trees: the aspen with their pale bark and quaking leaves, the pyramids of white fir whose blue-green needles were soft against her hand, in contrast to the sharp, stiff needles of the Colorado spruce trees, their branches nearly horizontal. She had a few of the Engleman spruce with their reddish, scaly bark, and several alders looking like large shrubs. Finally, there was a single box-elder sitting bowed and twisted at one corner of the lot, down on the steepest part of the slope, but still too high up to benefit from the winding stream below on someone else's land. Its leaves seemed tentative and final, its wood weak, past its life span. It was, of course, the tree she loved best, and she spent hours caressing and memorising the gestures of its branches, even though it was the hardest to get to and the trip back up the incline to her cabin left her breathless and dazed.

The names of the species, or the numbers of each, hardly mattered. It was the characters of the individual trees which interested her, and all that would matter when her ordinary sight was gone. With every walk she gradu-ally etched the map to each one into her tired and slowly shrinking brain, and after dark, when she finally lay down and practiced the blindness to come, she could see them like old neighbours standing at the ends of their paths, her feet making a different dance as she visited each one at its particular nexus of rock and sand, slope and plain.

After her first week in this new world her daughters came to visit, Ellen with her rambunctious twin girls and Susan with her pale, shy son, so much like his mother and so special just in the way he gazed at everything new, tilt-ing his head now and then to get a better, more magical view. Of course she was pleased to see them, even when their fascination did not match hers as she gave them the grand tour.

"This hill is just way too steep for you, mother!" Ellen said, spreading her feet ever wider apart as Liz guided them down, all in a ragged, nodding line like quail. Liz supposed Ellen meant to give herself balance through a wider stance, but Ellen's jerking stride and exaggerated expressions only made her mother laugh.

The twins raced past, down the slope to the elder, panicking their mother to squeals and creasing their grandmother's face with a smile. Once there they seemed bored and disappointed, but Susan's boy permitted Liz to guide his hand in and around the arthritic limbs, feeling the frozen reach of the elder's brittle stand. "It's almost like a poem," she told him, "but without the words."

As they all followed her the rest of the afternoon it was Susan who first commented on the new and slow deliberation of her mother's pace. "Mom, are you having trouble walking? Is it your arthritis in this mountain air?"

"I bet it's her breathing," Ellen said. "I noticed you were having difficulty earlier, climbing back up the slope. It's the thin air, isn't it, Mother? You're not getting enough oxygen."

Liz tried to explain to her daughters her methodology, and the map she was trying to create so slowly in her mind. She tried to explain to them the importance of this work, for that inevitable time when her eyes became no more than polished stones, and although she could see they made an honest and loving effort to understand what she was saying, she could also see that they weren't quite there yet, and she would be making this journey alone.

Ellen insisted on making a doctor's appointment for her later in the week to investigate this new limitation in her mobility. She smiled and agreed, knowing that she would be calling the doctor's office in the morning to cancel. But for now she allowed them to say goodbye, happy that they had a plan for helping her.

By the end of the fourth month she could differentiate every tree by posture, attitude, and something invisible she could identify only as "presence". By the end of the sixth month she had individual, particular names for about half of them. By the end of nine months she had appropriately named them all. After a year and a half she could visit each one with her eyes closed.

Her children's visits remained constant, and for the most part pleasant. They had largely given up trying to woo her from her new world. She permitted regular visits from a nurse with one of the mountain clinics, and her daughters arranged for a steady stream of supplies.

Her eyesight continued to worsen and sometimes the incremental losses and resulting necessary adjustments frightened her. Every month it seemed she was forced to make some new, unplanned exploration, and maps were not always available.

Still, the trees made good company. They seemed to have no intentions of moving, even though her process of getting to them wasn't always exactly the same. It reassured her that visiting them during the day and visiting them at night—lying down, her eyes closed, dreams waiting—was pretty much the same.

The fire came one afternoon out of the west as she sat on a rock waiting for a breeze to stroke her face and unravel her hair. Instead she smelled the smoke and heard the change as it swept across the ridge ahead of her. She wasn't sure what she should do, but staying outside seemed unwise. She took a few moments to check the old elder as she had done every day since moving here. Its survival seemed as unlikely as ever, but still it drank water, still it made leaves.

The trip back up the slope was even worse than ever, the pain of her breathing made sharper by the smoke. Once inside she shut doors and windows tight and stuffed towels into the gaps where she could. Then she called the sheriff. He said he'd send someone for her. She said there must be others, children perhaps, who needed him more, so he should wait. He said, "Don't be foolish, Liz. You're blind."

She opened the door only once before the deputy's car arrived. That was because she was sure she could hear her trees screaming. What met her at the edge of the porch was heat, a fierce blue and yellow demon with great liquid eyes and massive flowing hair consuming her dark and beautiful world.

Her cabin was saved. She did not believe them until she was able to step back inside it. She cried for relief then; they had not lied to her. But the trees were all gone, they said. She asked them to describe what they saw, but after several poor attempts they had to apologise. They said that one old elder near the edge of the property had not burned completely but it could not possibly survive. She did not bother to correct them.

She appreciated that her daughters did not attempt to persuade her to move. They visited more frequently for a time, and talked about the new seedlings they had ordered for the land, and how they were actually looking forward to helping plant them, under her supervision, of course. Her grandchildren talked animatedly of their young lives, filling her head with exciting, colourful pictures, and told her their own ideas for what plants they might put around the cabin, and pictures came with these ideas as well.

She thanked them all, and it was truly a wonderful thing. And she did not remind them that she wouldn't likely live long enough to witness the results. Before they left her they pulled her rocking chair out on the porch as she requested. Ellen expressed one small worry that with constant motion the runners might creep out over the steps and tip her over, but when everyone else objected she let it drop.

It was many months before the smoke dissipated completely and even after that there was always a trace. Whether that ghost of smoke was embedded in the land or simply hard pressed into her memory she was never quite sure. But soon enough she was breathing the green and the breeze and the insect chatter. The sun was warmer on her face now with no trees to block it. Now and then she even ventured down the slope to caress the prayerful aspect of the lone box elder and make her way breathlessly back up the slope over the paths to companions who no longer lived there.

And every night, early, after dinner was over and as soon as she could, she lay down under that grand sweep of trees, now a forest, now a wood, a dark and endless grove densely populated with trunk alongside trunk, each tree named and in its own place on her ancient map, showing her the way down that dim lane toward home.

Smoke in a Bottle

Daddy had the five beer bottles, their labels peeled off, lined up on the shelf. Then he puffed and puffed on his cigarette, packing the smoke into his mouth, making his eyes go funny because that was part of the show. Moving fast he put his mouth over each bottle, filled it with smoke, capped it with an old bottle cap, moved to the next. When he was done he had five bottles full of smoke.

He held each one in front of the fire, turning it so that the smoke flowed, curled inside, made patterns, made faces, weird shapes dancing. Then he'd flip off the cap and the smoke escaped as fast as anything, leaving behind a little stink, that was all.

"Smoke in a bottle, kids," he'd say. "That's all it is. Just like people."

Then he'd sway like a ruined house in a hurricane wind, and sometimes he'd stagger around the room. We knew Christmas was over when Dad fell into the Christmas tree.

So maybe Dad didn't fall into the Christmas tree every year. Maybe it was only seven or eight years out of ten. But fall he did, and although it made our mother every way of being angry and frustrated, it made us kids laugh every time, even when he broke something. He was a man of simple entertainments, using the things he always had with him—cigarettes and beer bottles mostly, and a damaged sense of balance—but his act always worked with us.

I hadn't been back in St. Charles in twenty years. Not because I hated it. When you live in a place as poor as that people think you must hate it and you can't wait to leave. I knew I was poor but I didn't know I was that poor. I got fed and I lived in the prettiest, greenest place I've ever known—southwest Virginia. Did you know the early Indians called Lee County "Paradise"?

As my cheap rental car rounded the bend I thought the town was on fire. Grey clouds drifted along the road, piled up in front of the car, broke apart and ran away. I rolled my window down and realised it was just morning mist, but there was this sharp scent that burned the nose, like cigarette smoke.

I drove slowly into town. The road had been patched so much it looked like an asphalt quilt. I'd kept a picture of the town in my memory but from the looks of things big chunks were missing, buildings cut out, blown away, replaced by weeds, worn out trailers, and a few hollow stores leaning like dozing drunks. No signs of Christmas, no lights, no street decorations.

In the forties and fifties St. Charles had thousands of people, with restaurants and stores and even a small movie theatre. The valley's narrow there, so they built everything down close to the highway. A concrete sidewalk on each side didn't leave much room for road. On Saturday nights the road shrank down to one lane and you could barely get through. You could hear the party all through the valley, or so Daddy used to tell us. By my time in the late sixties St. Charles was falling asleep.

Daddy drank a lot and worked only occasionally. These days you'd call him an alcoholic. I didn't know that word when I was a kid.

I knew there was still a lot good about the town, but it's not the kind of place you come back to. No jobs to speak of since the mines shut down. And part of getting older is looking back and understanding how much you didn't have.

The first Christmas I remember from elementary school we had to draw names and get a present for one of our classmates. The night before the party our mother sat the three of us down and handed us each a pack of chewing gum and helped us wrap them up fancy in a cloth package with dress ribbon and a quilting square. She showed us how to hold the scissors and where to cut the cloth and how to split and fold the ribbon until at the end we had three unique flowers attached to these beautiful little packages.

Because the girl I gave the gum to had been brought up right, she made herself smile when she thanked me politely. But I knew exactly what disappointment looked like. At the end of the day I saw her talking to her mom and showing the gum. Her mom looked at me then, not in a mean way but like she was measuring me for a suit. That was the first time I ever felt really poor.

Dad died from lung disease shortly after my freshman year in college and I went home for his funeral; I came back again for my sister's wedding. And this last time for my mother's funeral while I was going through a divorce. That good woman never even met my kids. Three times in all those years. I'm not proud of that.

The house had been sold to an investor. When my brother and sister asked me if I could clean it out, I agreed, even though that was the last thing I wanted to do for Christmas. It was the least I could do. I wasn't going to see my kids until after the holiday anyway. You could say a lot bad about my dad, but at least he was there every Christmas.

Our old house had lost most of its yard and the sheltering trees, and a tangle of weeds and rusted metal hugged the foundation. I parked where my mother's flower beds used to be. Inside, the light was yellow from weak lamps and sun burning through brittle shades, dust over every-thing, as if some of that amber light had disintegrated into a thick layer of brown. I felt like holding my breath—it was like trying to breathe inside a grave. I wondered if this was anything like what my dad experienced all those years ago while his lungs were failing.

In one room I counted six cheap headboards, nine sets of bed-springs, a box full of wheels, two rotting pillows jammed into the corner, a dark, viscous stain on the top one. All would go in the trash.

The smallest bedroom was empty, except for some mud and grease on the floor. This had been Ann's. She was the youngest and always had the smallest room. My bedroom was a long, narrow room along the back of the house, like a closet. It still had a tiny little bookcase. I couldn't really find myself in that room, but I did re-member that bookcase. It had never held more than a few books. One Christmas my mother had given me two—*The Adventures of Robin Hood* and *The Legends of King Arthur*. She couldn't have paid much, but she'd been so happy to give them to me. I'd read them over and over until they fell apart.

My brother's room was just an empty box. Mom and Daddy's room was on the other side of the house. This was where my mother died. It still had her bed, her dress-er, her night table, a picture of an Indian in a canoe on the wall. It still looked like a real room, like she'd just stepped out to pick flowers for the dinner table.

I smelled cigarette smoke. I looked around and saw the brown silhouette on the shade, the figure outside sway-ing, probably drunk, struggling to hold onto his ciga-rette. By the time I got outside he was gone.

I looked across the yard at my neighbour's house: a man standing on the porch, smoking.

"Can I help you?" I could hear my voice shaking.

"Don't need no help."

"Were you just in my yard?"

"Nosir. Is that your yard?"

"My mother lived here."

"Hey! Hey, Willie? Is that you?"

After I grabbed some chairs, my old friend Eddie and I sat in the empty living room, mostly just staring at each other. We'd both changed a lot, Eddie more visibly. He weighed about half what he once had, and he had tattoos, and about half a goatee, as if something had eaten the right side of it. Eddie finally broke the silence with "So, you got any beers?"

I carried the six-pack in from the car. I gave him the whole thing.

"You're not drinking?"

"Not tonight," I said. Actually I almost never drink. I had no idea why I'd bought the beer. "Just give me the empties."

He stared at the bottles dubiously. "What? They collectible?"

"No. I just thought I'd put them on that shelf over the fireplace, like Dad used to."

He squinted at the thin piece of wood. "I remember that. Hope they don't fall off—looks a little crooked." He started on the first one, and then stopped, raising it in my direction. "Merry Christmas." He drank a few swallows, then said, "Your dad fell into the Christmas tree one year, didn't he?"

"Six or seven years, actually."

"Yeah. I remember laughing about it. There were some years I wish my family had had something like that to laugh about. But six or seven times? Even if you're drinking heavy, that's kind of, unusual."

We didn't talk much after that—just the occasional burst of words, with long periods of silence in between. I didn't mind—that was what a conversation was in St. Charles. He'd tell me something about his life now, and he'd tell me about some classmate or other, who had died, divorced, or disappeared from that part of the country, never to be seen again. Periodically he'd hand me an empty beer bottle and I'd scrape the label off and balance it on the shelf.

As the night wore on I moved the old lamps from my mother's room in for more light, but the best I could accomplish was a few bright patches of brilliance and a great deal of dirty shadow that seemed to float along the walls and over the ceiling, making the house appear to sway, as if I were the one drinking. Eddie, on the other hand, seemed like the sober one, talking more as the hours passed of people and events I'd largely forgotten.

"You remember Jack Gilford, don't you?"

"Sure. Is he dead, too?"

"No, but he oughta be," Eddie said, giggling. "A mite cold in here, don't you think? Why don't you start something in that fireplace?"

I was surprised to find about an inch of snow on the ground. *You got snow, you're a rich man,* was something Daddy used to say. I'd understood that even as a kid. Snow was good for covering up shabbiness, and ugliness, and essentials missing. It even had a way of transforming those things into something quaint, suitable for a picture postcard.

I looked across the valley at the pinpricks of light floating down like slow-falling stars, and the steam from chimneys floating up, columns like vague figures standing on rooftops, watching. I couldn't see the main road from our old house, but I could hear the busy traffic and all those people.

I stopped moving. What was I thinking? Those noises were from another time, and I couldn't be hearing them now. It had to be some distortion in the air that had caused the effect, some echo off the stripped-to-rock hills. I heard coughing, a drawn-out wheeze. I went to the edge of the window and peeked inside. Eddie was peacefully drinking, head tilted back and lips around the bottle's mouth. And I heard the wheeze again, followed by the bone-rattling cough. I looked around. A few yards away a man stood with his back to me, wearing nothing out there in the cold but a T-shirt and boxer shorts. He coughed again, his whole body shaking, hunched shoulders seeming to broaden, as if in advance of some transformation. I ran a couple of feet to the wall and grabbed some wood stacked there, ran inside without looking back. I bumped against the wall in my haste and one of the beer bottles tumbled to the floor into an explosion of glass. "Sorry," I said.

"No biggie, bro. I'll have a replacement for you in just a sec."

I said nothing to Eddie about what I had seen and heard. I built a fire—it was a little smoky, there was probably debris blocking part of the chimney. But we tolerated it, even though it made us cry a little. After Eddie left there were scattered voices in the smoke, but I learned to tolerate them as well.

Early next morning Eddie showed up with a serious face, dragging a small white pine nailed to a crude base of crossed scrap wood. "Christmas Eve, Willie. I reckon you need a tree." He grinned then, and in the burning glare off the snow I saw that he had numerous missing teeth. "Don't worry—I didn't steal it. It was in my back yard."

Eddie left to spend the next several days with family in Tennessee. I dragged the tree in and put it in the corner of the living room, sat down in a chair and spent some time staring at it. It leaned quite a bit, but still managed to stay up. I decided then to find something to put on it—I knew I'd feel even worse about the day if I left it bare.

I hadn't been down in the cellar since we found that rat the size of a beaver when I was nine years old. The rats used to scrabble out of the abandoned mines and sneak into town. About the only way to get rid of them was a shotgun. But that's where my mother always kept the tree decorations, and anything else she didn't want us kids to mess with.

The light fixture still worked, but it was like a candle at the opening of a mine. Inside it smelled like rotting vegetables and spoiled meat. The invisible walls were lined with mason jars whose dark contents absorbed just enough light to make me avoid them. I found the damp cardboard box with the decorations halfway in, pulling it close even as something scurried out of it. To my credit I didn't drop the box, but hurried upstairs and shoved it by the tree.

After a couple of years of Dad wiping out the Christmas tree, my mother had put her favourite decorations on the shelf by the beer bottles rather than risk them. There the glass angel and the ceramic deer and the little Santa Claus had had a perfect view of Dad's mysterious smoking bottles. I didn't need to be so cautious, and nestled them right into the front branches where I could see them. None of the coloured lights lit reliably, so I didn't bother with them. But I did discover that lighting a fire in the fireplace created interesting reflections in the shiny coloured balls and fragments of icicle I scraped out of the bottom of the box. Shards of rainbow swam in the walls as an untraceable draft lightly stirred the branches. I wished my kids could see it.

I wasn't even sure what we'd gotten the kids for Christmas that year. Since they were all going to be at her parents' house she'd handled everything, and I hadn't even asked.

This tree had no presents under it, but there had never been many presents under the tree in this house.

I must have dozed off, and when I woke up I was sure I'd caught the house on fire—I smelled burning—wood and plastic, paper and cloth, a world of things turned to smoke and drifting into my nose and mouth. I gaped at the fireplace, my eyes blurry.

On the shelf smoke boiled in and out of the remaining bottles. I walked over for a better view: although smoke carved the air in all five, in the two on the end it swirled into miniature, fiery galaxies before floating up the necks and out into the room where they joined the shadows flowing across the ceiling.

I could hear a soft wheeze behind me, but I could not bring myself to turn around. Instead I walked into my mother's old bedroom and went to sleep on her oval rug.

I found the Christmas tree lying on the floor the next morning, a great dent on the ceiling-facing side, branches pushed aside and broken as if from a great weight.

It's funny how sometimes you have all the evidence right in front of you, and yet it takes you years to give it the proper importance. A man doesn't accidentally fall into a Christmas tree seven out of ten years even if he is a drunk. And his wife doesn't just put up with that kind of behaviour. It had all been an act for the benefit of my brother, my sister, and me. I remembered how in those years, when we kids got practically nothing on Christmas morning, Dad always told his best stories and did his best tricks to entertain us, to distract us. And we couldn't help but laugh when he swayed and stumbled and fell into that poor, blameless tree.

There on the shelf were the glass angel and the ceramic deer and the little Santa Claus, safe as houses.

Christmas was over. I spent the day cleaning and throwing the remaining pieces of that old life away (save three ornaments). The next day I would drive to the coast and see my kids.

Est Enim Magnum Chaos

Sometimes he felt so terribly close that if he viewed the passage from here to there at a slightly different angle, or traced a shadow a little further in search of the reality which cast it, or if he only had the patience to listen to one more word of the conversation, he would at last find the edge of the world that disappointed, and the world that promised so much.

The envelope had no return address, and contained only a small slip of paper bearing a scribble of illegible words as if written in a barely-controlled hand, like that of a weak elderly person. After a time Clarence decided it said, *Est enim magnum chaos*, but only because that was what he'd expected it to say. "For there is a great void." The message the five of them had agreed to send to one another if they arrived at the other side, at last in the infinite and real.

He paused in the short entrance passage, vaguely thinking that someone had gone out just as he'd come in, someone on a very different schedule, although his own schedule had been highly variable since retiring from the library.

In the antique mirror so incongruous in his modern tri-level, he saw reflections of an older house and the man who had lived there, leaving, just the back of his head with more hair than Clarence himself had ever had.

A creaking came from the room beyond the kitchen, but this house had no creaks, and no room beyond the kitchen. For a moment everything doubled, but the doubles seemed nothing like their originals, and then he could see properly again, the slip of paper with its simple sentence shaking in his hand as if alive. He took it to the small table where he kept his mail, but he was afraid to set it down. The surface was already full of notes he'd written to himself to remind himself of important things because he couldn't manage to keep it all in his head. Since he couldn't read his own handwriting anymore the notes had become useless. But he still wrote them.

The agreement had been a school boy's pact, even though they'd made it when they were all well into their fifties. It had been John's idea.

"We don't want to be those old men reading the obituaries every day and attending each other's funerals." This was after the bookseller Tom Gleason died, older than the rest by fifteen years. It had been their mutual friendship with Tom that had initially gathered them together. Tom had suggested the regular meetings for dinner, movies, the symphony, and spiritual discussions. Sometimes they would go to a play, but the plays had to be vetted by a trusted source. "There is no cultural calamity worse than a bad play," had been Tom's take.

Tom had been their number six, and the first of the group to die. By his request John and Clarence were pallbearers. Clarence had been quite touched by the honour.

"Is this what we're going to be doing the rest of our lives," John had continued, "waiting for each other to die? I've seen it before with men of a certain age. They stop serious discussion and fill their conversations with a catalogue of ailments."

"That's certainly not what I want," Raymond said. "I come here to discuss mystical issues, the possibilities of another world, not the dread of leaving this one." As always, he seemed full of complaint, but it usually required some effort to pry out the specifics.

"Illness is dull stuff," Ian said. "I suppose it's theoretically of great interest to the one who is ill." He paused for an uncomfortable length of time. "But I have never found that to be the case."

"But I suppose if one of us were in the process of . . . leaving," Everett said, "and were to, well, provide a narrative, that might fall within our usual topics."

They waited for Clarence to say something, and their patience was appreciated, but he also felt pressured. "I don't think I'd want that," he finally said. "I want to remember you all as you are now. Inquisitive. Perennial students. I'd want to know if anything happened to you, but I wouldn't care to watch it happen."

"Precisely." John laid out his suggestion. If one of them fell ill he would, if possible, send notice that he would not attend their get-togethers until his health improved.If he never returned then the others would know what had happened. "But," John smiled over his idea, "if one of us should achieve that which we all desire, and by some means step across the void into that truer reality we have been discussing, he will send a note stating, '*Est enim magnum chaos*'. From the Machen story, of course."

"Of course." Everett was always first to assert his understanding of any point. Clarence had nodded with the others, although he'd had serious reservations.

But this envelope had included no return address, which violated their agreement. What good was the message if he had no notion as to who had sent it?

Now and then in his junk mail were the pleas for contact from family members he'd never had, invitations to unfamiliar events, misdelivered correspondence he invariably opened. What if he were to answer one of these way-ward pieces? The notion made him vaguely sick.

Poor Ian was dead within the year. Apparently he'd been failing for some time. "Something we might have known, if we had more women in our lives," had been John's opinion. Each member of the group had received a letter from a lawyer, the firm's name and address printed in banknote quality on the front. Inside, on equally-impressive letterhead, had been the one line, crisply typed: *Est enim magnum chaos.*

"I don't understand," Everett had said. "Does he require a lawyer to communicate from the other side?" It sounded like a tasteless joke, but Everett had no sense of humour.

"I suspect Ian left a scattering of confused instructions. Not to dwell on specifics, but he may have been in some pain. An overzealous lawyer, intent on completeness—"

"And billable hours," Raymond interjected.

"And billable hours to the estate," John continued, "might have confused his notes concerning our agreement as instructions to send each of us that message upon Ian's death. I'd suggest we simply ignore them." There had been general agreement, but Clarence had still kept his copy, tucked into a shoebox of things he did not completely understand.

John himself had been the next to leave their group, but he had disappointed them by thoroughly violating the spirit of the agreement. They'd all received fine linen envelopes one day, his name and business printed in a perfect density of blue: "Valuations & Expert Advice".

They hadn't seen him in months, and given the nature of their arrangement they'd assumed him either disabled or ill, although they'd all been hesitant to say. Then Clarence saw John on a television program with his pretty young wife discussing antiques as investment opportunities. They soon became aware of his numerous other local media ventures—a radio show, a talk to "seniors", even a regular column in the regional weekly.

Inside that fine envelope had been an equally fine business card, inscribed elegantly on one side with *Est enim magnum chaos*. On the other side was printed John's name, and written in crowded pencil the notation, "Many thanks, but I no longer have time to attend your gatherings." He had no idea how the others felt, but Clarence, to his surprise, had been practically devastated.

Clarence continued to hold the scribbled note with that promising phrase in his hand, rubbing it between his fingers, closing his eyes. A recent onset of mild neuropathy made it difficult for him to feel that there was anything between his fingers at all. But for the moment he imagined it as a kind of key, this world gradually fading with his rubbing and the next emerging among its fibres. All of us, he thought, have the power to make different choices. He'd written himself a note concerning that very idea at some point or other; he imagined he still had it. He wished he could have given that advice to his younger self. He wished he could have explained what he'd be missing. He held up the paper again for examination.

This version of the inscription was far from John's level of elegance or depth of uncongeniality. The paper looked much older than the writing, creased and rubbed thin, and the handwriting troubled, as if the words had been put down with great emotion. He would have loved to compare this note to those received by the others, but of course now there were no others. Had their notes been sent out anyway? It was a strange notion.

He dropped the note onto an old Chinese lacquered tray he kept on the sideboard. This was where he put any sort of correspondence he hadn't figured out how to deal with: insurance papers, legal forms, the rare social invitations. An announcement for his fiftieth high school reunion had sat in the tray two years before he'd finally thrown it out.

He'd bought the tray from John down in that little shop he'd opened a year before his death. Divorced, frail, and his local media celebrity a distant memory, John had saddened him deeply in their final meeting.

He went back to his little mail table. Several of his notes had fallen to the floor, and behind the legs, against the wall. That sort of thing was always happening—he had so many notes—but he rarely noticed, or did anything about it. This time he stooped and gathered them up, and tried to make neat little stacks on the table. He really ought to sort through them, arrange them, perhaps throw some away, but he knew he never would. Even if he couldn't understand what he'd written on most of them, they must have been important at the time. If he started throwing them out he might lose some valuable information.

Clarence went down to his nook to read. One corner in the lower level featuring a tall vertical window from floor to ceiling, it looked out on a spare bit of garden, a variety of flowers and a vine-laden fence, a few large stones hauled away from the garden of his old home and deposited here at too much expense. On the other side of that fence was the parking lot of a high-rise for young commuters, but he couldn't see above the fence when seated in his comfortable high-backed reading chair so he could pretend a kind of well-manicured seclusion.

Sometimes he imagined there was a door in his back fence he could use for exploring. Perhaps someday he would have one put in.

He glanced at the bookcase crammed with books and journals. Here and there a long note obtruded between two volumes. Other notes had gathered like dead moths in the dust-laden tops of the books. Some had spilled out and lay pressed against the base of the bookcase.

Raymond had never really forgiven him for selling the old house. It had been a convenient rallying point before their dinner outings, and the kind of house they all loved: pre-1900 with tall ceilings, plentiful woodwork, numerous bookcases, and stuffy dust-laden air to insulate them from the present-day. But it had also been drafty and encumbered with a torturous set of stairs, and the cost of heating it had been prohibitive on a retirement income. A move into a smaller, more manageable house in the older suburbs seemed the wisest course. Raymond, an inner city loyalist, felt betrayed.

"Your nook may feel like a gentleman's study, but it's all illusory with that monstrosity towering next door."

"My old house was only a block from a major highway. All I had to do was step outside to see, hear, and smell it."

"At least it was Victorian."

"Well, someday these tri-levels, too, will seem quite quaint. It's a comfortable home, Raymond, one that I can afford, and a block from a branch library."

Raymond should have been more grateful, since Clarence had given him a large number of books as he disposed of things for the move. Raymond acted as if he were saving them from Clarence's willful neglect. Raymond died six months later; Clarence wondered sometimes who had those books now.

Clarence and Everett had not seen Raymond for a time, and then Clarence ran into Raymond's daughter at the local library sale where she had just dropped off a large donation. Clarence noticed some of his own old books in the boxes, but did not mention it.

He felt embarrassed when she recognised him and walked over.

"Excuse me; you're Clarence Mayhew, aren't you?"

"Yes. You're Sarah, Raymond's daughter, I believe? He showed me your photograph once."

She paused, looking troubled. "Did you know he died three months ago?"

Clarence felt the sudden grip of shame. He thought, we considered the possibility, but didn't tell her. "No, I'm so sorry. I hadn't heard."

"I was surprised, you know? I'd always thought that you and the others were his best friends—he certainly spent a great deal of time with you over the years. But in the funeral instructions he left, it stated specifically that the group of you wouldn't be coming, and weren't to be informed. Not that you weren't invited, mind you, just that, somehow you weren't to be expected. What, was there a falling out of some kind?"

"Oh, no, no. Nothing like that. We all liked Raymond very much. It was just that we all had this agreement about—this sort of thing."

"What kind of agreement?"

Again, the shame and embarrassment. And the belief that they had all acted so foolishly. "I'd really rather not say—I don't think I have the right. But your father was part of it—we all decided this together."

"Well, I'm sorry, but I just think it's a shame." She'd tried to smile for him, and walked away.

Perhaps he was being uncharitable, but Clarence didn't think Raymond had had it in him to send the note. Of all of them, he'd certainly seemed the least spiritual. The daughter was a possibility, he supposed, but not a very good one. Perhaps if she were angry enough, but unless she was a very good actor, she clearly didn't know about their arrangement.

He wished he'd never gone along with the others. Perhaps if he'd spoken up he could have dissuaded them. It might have made a small difference for all of them—they could have been there for each other.

Clarence walked over to his reading light to turn it on, settle into a good read for the afternoon. Reading had always distracted him, even during the worst of times. But he thought something had just come out of the chair and passed him, to allow him in. And despite the warm air by the window, the chair seat was cold and unpleasant.

He heard a soft crinkling noise as he sat down. He stood up quickly, and found that the chair was covered with notes. He picked up a few—on each the hasty scrawl of a line appeared to be in some foreign language. He angrily brushed them off the seat; he'd sweep them up later.

It was odd thinking of Raymond with a grown daughter, particularly one willing to talk to Clarence that way. Raymond himself would have been far more indirect. What had the man's wife been like? She would have had to be forceful; it would have been difficult to get anything done around the house otherwise.

Not that Clarence himself would have been an easy husband. He'd come close to marriage years ago, and then she'd moved across country to care for her ill sister's children. His letters to her had been long, and no doubt obsessive. She'd responded now and then, complaining that she couldn't read them. She'd asked if he could type his letters to her, but it had been his feeling back then that personal letters should never be typed. They'd eventually lost touch, and he hadn't tried again.

He'd seen far too many disappointed marriages where the couples had made do with their second choices, or third. And a disappointing marriage seemed a terrible thing, another agreement he did not think he could bear.

If he could have sent the person he'd been then a message regarding the lifelong consequences of that way of thinking, he would have.

He heard a creaking again, this time on the steps up to the bedroom. He walked slowly up the stairs. Shadows climbed ahead of him as the pattern of light and shade changed with each shift in perspective, and he wasn't sure if it was just his own footsteps he was hearing or a twinning of footsteps slightly unsynchronised. He began to feel dizzy, and made it to the bed just in time, closing his eyes and waiting for the sensation to pass. The air appeared to revolve around him, the geometry compromised.

He considered the possibility that this was what death was like, the transitioning of forms, the metamorphosis of actor into memory. In a kind of physics people created disturbances in the field, and disturbances had to be controlled. He regretted not having tried to be someone else, to play some other part. A different speech made at the proper time, a shift in diet or style, might have changed everything. New viewpoints were possible.

Everett's wife had visited him six months ago. When she'd shown up at his door he'd had no idea who she was. He hadn't even known Everett had a wife.

"I know of your agreement," she said. "So I realised you wouldn't know. But I thought—" She'd paused and he felt sorry for her. She seemed so kind, and yet Everett had never mentioned her.

"I appreciate your coming to tell me in person," he said.

"Oh, he talked about you all the time. He loved you very much."

Clarence felt his facial muscles stiffen to hold a polite smile. Love? Surely not. He had no idea what to say. What was there to say? Was she just being nice, or had Everett lied to her? Everett had never acted the least bit admiring.

But it certainly was no secret that so many people possessed a quiet heart.

Clarence had walked her to her bus stop. From some angles she resembled someone he might have known a long time ago. But the mind plays tricks, and sees with a kind of yearning. He'd wanted to ask her to stay awhile longer, but how would she have received such an invitation?

They were surrounded by trees and shadowed benches where people might sit and talk. He knew that all these had been transplanted from somewhere else, and the quaint stone walls recently built and artificially aged. But did this make the feelings they created any less real? He suspected that if he ever saw what truly lay beneath it all, he might despair.

He told her about the family-owned Thai restaurant up the street where he regularly dined. They knew him by name and always seemed glad to see him. The teenage daughters were kind and one patted his arm from time to time. The elder had earned a scholarship and everyone was very proud.

Stay, he thought, as he waved Everett's wife goodbye, please stay.

He had a notion that someone was painting his portrait as he lay in bed. They had some trouble getting the colours right. And he was restless, and kept moving. He supposed he was a very hard man to get a message to, or from.

Before he opened his eyes he felt a weight shift in the bed, and someone got up before him. He almost got a glimpse of them passing into the next room, but not quite.

He went back downstairs at last to read. The chair felt warm, and the air around him smelled slightly used and dusty with old books. He pulled out a volume of Machen from the bookcase—*Far Off Things*, one of the first books he'd bought from Tom. A Near Fine hardcover, the 1922 Martin Secker edition.

He remembered his inordinate affection at the time for the "Price 7/6 Net" printed on the spine of the slightly-chipped dust jacket. Inside the book he still had Tom's original hand-written sales receipt, on that old, smooth paper he'd used.

He got up and went to the Chinese lacquered tray, re-trieving the slip of paper with the Latin inscription he'd received in the mail that day. It was the same kind of paper. He held both pieces in his trembling hand. He looked again at the words, *Est enim* . . . He still could but barely read the words, but he recognised those e's. Tight and angular, with the loop narrowed practically to a line like an eye almost closed. The way he had always made his letter e.

He used to write lots of letters to people. Not so much anymore, not since his handwriting had deteriorated so severely. Most of his writing now, he thought, was to him-self, in the form of random, ultimately forgettable notes. But there would be no point in mailing these notes, cer-tainly, unless to get his own attention.

He pulled out volume after volume Tom had sold him. He looked at the receipts still inside. Many had been writ-ten on the back with his own, incommunicative hand-writing, no doubt concerning groceries he never bought, household tasks he'd never gotten around to doing. Re-minders, but he did not understand any of them.

He looked again at the note he'd received in the mail. He held it up to the light. Something had been written in pencil on the other side and then delicately erased. It might have been something important, something he needed to know. He thought he could detect an amount, then the tax that had been added. This had once been one of Tom's receipts.

He picked up the notes still scattered around the floor at his feet. The words were almost unreadable, but that might have been *magnum*; that other word might have been *chaos*. He could hear hesitant footsteps upstairs, a sighing that travelled the house and begged at the closed windows and doors.

Live alone long enough, everywhere you look there are signs you were there. Clarence had thought that once. Or had he merely read it and made it his own? Sometimes he wished he could communicate with who he once had been, who might have changed everything for who he was now.

He wondered if that might go both ways. Sometimes we forget everything we once knew. We need reminders.

Est enim magnum chaos. For there is a great void.

Perhaps he had always known this. He had no doubt it was true. But you need not face it alone. The experience need not be an endless fall.

These Days When All is Silver and Bright

All week the sky had been hazy, bright, a backlit silver that promised something, but she couldn't say what. There were thunderstorms in the west, with cracks of lightning. Trina had forgotten something, she knew, and had dumped her purse looking, but nothing had come to her out of her haze.

It was her second day working at the boutique, and she saw a little boy who looked exactly like her brother walking through the strip mall parking lot. Her eyes hurt looking through the glass, but she knew what she saw.

He could have been a look-alike—lots of six-year-old boys looked alike—but with the set of his shoulders, his hurry-to-catch-up walk, that odd shade of yellow hair that turned red in a certain accidental light, it had to be her little brother, wandering unsupervised. People raced their cars through the lot as if it were just another street. Every time a car passed she couldn't stop herself from shutting her eyes.

She wanted to call him in, or beat on the window to warn him. She held herself back. Certainly that was exactly the way Brian had looked at six, but that was twenty-two years ago.

Dinner was early. After the accident and she'd moved back in with her parents, they always had dinner early. Her dad said that gave her more time to rest. She really needed to get her own place again.

Brian passed the potatoes and smiled. "Tired, Sis?"

"She works too much, and so soon after the accident," her mother said.

"Don't hover, you two. Brian, it's always good to see you, but you've been over every night this week. Trina's doing fine, aren't you, Trina?" Her dad passed her the steak, even though she hadn't asked for it. She put one on her plate, but ignored it. She didn't like meat—why couldn't he see that? There was a bowl with tomato chunks in cottage cheese, a plate with broken sticks of bok choy, bits of walnut embedded in churned sweet potato. There was nothing here she could bear to look at, much less eat.

"Everybody, I'm fine. It was just a little accident." She gazed at the meat lying in its own juices. There was a gash, a tiny bubble of sauce. She laid her hand flat on the meat. It was as warm as her hand. She closed her eyes, and saw herself walking across the plate, kneeling, lying down over the meat, felt it warm, and then cool against her cheek.

She looked across the table at her mother who'd been crying. "I guess I'm tired. Thanks for having dinner early," she said, and went to her room.

One time she had hidden all of Brian's baseball cards, his most prized possessions. He'd cried himself to sleep. She had felt ashamed, but he'd always left them lying around. They'd been so slippery underfoot—he'd spilled them everywhere—it had been like sliding on oil.

That morning she helped a lady buy a winter coat for her son. She brought coats with more and more padding to try on the boy. He held his short arms up in the air while she pulled the sleeves over them. He looked like he was drowning in coat. The woman slipped the hood over his head and pulled the drawstring. Trina looked into the little hole made by the tightened hood. His eyes looked so big inside the hole, but he was okay. It made her smile. Little boys were like magic, until they weren't.

Her mother had left a container of pasta and tomato for her lunch, with a note that said, "You need to eat something." Trina poked at the pale noodles before dropping the container into the trash.

Out in the lot that little boy who looked like her brother ran between parked cars, arms stretched out, making noises like a falling airplane. Trina wanted to tell him to stop, but he never listened to her. She didn't know what she was doing. The sky glowed the colour of fish bellies waiting to be filleted. She closed her eyes against an approaching headache. Her mother screamed at her, the high-pitched sound of compressing air making her eyes fly open. The boy was floating high in the brightly polished sky, arms stretched out, swollen coat flapping in the wind, beginning to come apart, the pieces of it falling away. Her mother would be so angry—she never watched him closely enough.

"There are some things you should never see. If you see them, you'll never be the same again." Her mother was always giving her advice that she already knew, or was too late to be useful. She'd closed her eyes again, afraid to open them.

Trina fell asleep at the dinner table. "I told you it was too soon. Just look." That was her mother, but she didn't know if she was speaking to her or to her dad. "I don't know why you let her take that job at that mall. I never go there anymore—I didn't think she would, either." Her mother sounded angry. She was always making her mother angry. But everything would be okay as long as her mother didn't scream.

"It was her choice—she's a grown woman. I thought maybe it would help her." He talked more, but Trina couldn't remember.

She woke up sometime in the night. Someone was crying. Her face was wet, so it might be her. She listened some more, felt her mouth. Someone else was crying down the hall, but she was crying as well.

Her room was so empty. No pictures. All of her old things gone. Didn't she used to collect toys? She vaguely remembered all kinds of toys.

If she'd ever stop crying. She could hear herself, sounding as if her heart were breaking. It hurt Trina to hear herself. She went to the bathroom for a pill. She didn't find a pill, but she found her mother's door open. Her mother sat with her back to the door crying with a sound like things breaking. A familiar photo album lay open on her lap with photos of that little boy from the parking lot who looked so much like Brian when he was that age. Trina didn't like to think of it as a family resemblance, but as a family difference, like looking into a bad mirror under a hot sun—it hurt to see the faces. She really needed to get her own place again. There were some things a person just wasn't meant to see.

Trina got written up the next day because she spent so much time out in the parking lot. Every time business got slow she went out there. But she kept seeing that little boy who wasn't her brother running in and out between the parked cars under the white melting sun, and she just wanted to tell him to stop. She wanted to go find that kid's mother and tell her to pay more attention and keep her little boy safe.

Trina was sent home from work early and that was pretty embarrassing because her dad was going to have a thousand questions for her. But when she got home Brian was there.

He put his arms around her and hugged her tightly, and he was so tall—she'd almost forgotten how tall he was. His golden yellow hair—now fading into lemon, into something sadder than lemon—fell across his face.

She and Brian sat in her bedroom by themselves. "So how are you doing, Sis?"

"You're staying for dinner, aren't you?" she asked, trying not to cry, but she was pretty sure he was going to be leaving again. "Don't let Dad scare you away."

"Dad's okay. He was right, I've been hanging around too much—what did he call it? Hovering. But I just wanted to see how you were getting along, living here again with them, and everything." He glanced around. "Where's all your old stuff, anyway? Did Mom and Dad move your stuff somewhere?"

"I thought you took it. Most of those toys were yours, anyway. By the way, I'm sorry about your baseball cards, but you really shouldn't have left them lying around like that." Brian stared at her. She leaned over and tried to whisper. "Please stay for dinner. But I don't want to have meat again. There are just some things a person isn't meant to see."

They let her come back to work the next day, which was a good thing. It wasn't a great job but she needed to save enough to get her own place again. She couldn't remember much about that place, but Brian said she'd moved there right after graduation. He said she'd sworn off men after what happened with that guy in high school, and she just wanted to make their lives better. She just wished she knew where all her old stuff was.

She got so busy helping mothers buy their kids new clothes, getting squirmy little boys who looked like somebody's little brother in and out of jackets, that she didn't think to look out in the parking lot at all. Then her manager told her to take a lunch break and get out of there and walk around because she was making everybody nervous; and first thing, when she stepped out into that bright and silver day, she started thinking about that little boy.

She began searching the parking lot and even though the fact that he wasn't there probably meant his mother was finally taking good care of him, it made her scared. She had to hold her head down with her hand blocking the glare and searched the shadows between cars. She hated getting so close to the slimy tyres and the wet pavement, but that's where she knew she had to look. Cars were honking at her—maybe she had wandered too close to traffic.

She couldn't find him in the parking lot so she marched down the line of stores, looking into every window, walking right past the kids' clothing boutique even though lunch time was over, hiding her face from the pain-filled sky until she got to the store at the end of the strip mall. She looked inside and saw all those little boys and all those toys and not enough parents paying attention.

Screeching like an airplane falling out of the sky. She turned her head and there was that sweet little boy racing around the corner of the building with a model airplane held high up in his outstretched hand, his mouth wide open making sounds like a dying airplane.

Trina looked and saw the backs of the two women— one older and one younger passing a cigarette—not even watching because they just couldn't live if they saw what happened next. She ran hard but already the air was whistling, the pressure wanting to make her head explode. After everything started to pop and his bright yellow hair began to fill with liquid, she came face to face with the giant truck rising up on its shock absorbers and bearing its silver grill to scream at her as there, under the terrible tyres, her lovely son disassembled and vanished before her aching head. She only wished she'd had something in her hands then when she brought them up to cover her eyes.

Telling

Before he met Maggie, he thought he understood the difference between sense and nonsense. By the end, and he could smell it coming—redolent of fish and sweaty sheets—he could hardly tell the difference between breath and flesh.

They had visited three, four hundred houses for sale. They had driven down every street in the county, every nameless lane. They had done this in late October, with a layer of ice-capped snow on the ground, the wind low but steady enough to scour the back of your throat until you were made inarticulate.

Wayne did not complain, but it was painful, creeping along those shaded lanes, enduring the stares of suspicious neighbours, as the ice cracked and exploded beneath his tyres. It might have been better if he'd had any idea what she was looking for, but she did not share her criteria. Wayne supposed that was what artists were like. But it exhausted the people who loved them.

In most cases a relatively slow drive-by was sufficient: the house would apparently be in the wrong architectural style, or too tall, or too wide. He wasn't permitted to say anything—he couldn't even hum while he was driving. And now and then she would insist that they step inside, or walk around, or lie on the floor and gaze at the ceiling. Wayne had been unemployed two years, but he did have his real estate license, and for once that made him feel useful.

Wayne didn't enjoy any of it. He especially didn't enjoy lying on those dusty floors, looking into those crusty ceilings, inviting dust into his eyes, dust into his mouth, where it tasted aspirin bitter, like all that was left by the end of the day, like the end of life itself.

He had no idea why they were doing it, except Maggie said it was something she needed to do before she could choose the right house. And as much as she annoyed and infuriated him, Wayne adored Maggie, and would do anything she asked.

"This is the one," she said. "Finally, this is the one. I can feel it."

The house was in worse shape than most of the others.

Unpainted grey boards pushed through tatters of off-white colour. Inside, the walls were thin as paper. Wayne imagined he could see the colours of the next room bleeding through.

"If you dropped something you'd hear it in every room of the house." As if on cue, vague, hesitant sounds travelled from the other end of the house, or farther.

Maggie hadn't heard or ignored them. "But that's a good thing, isn't it? Nothing can ever sneak up on you."

The fact that something sneaking up was even a consideration appalled him. "It smells funny in here," he said. "Are you sure you can live in a place that smells funny?"

"They make paint with chemicals that kill the odour."

And that was that. She'd made up her mind. He supposed she didn't care how the place smelled. For him it was as if he'd crawled inside a loaf of old, damp bread. The rich stink filled the nose and spilled over into the mouth. He imagined a sponginess in the wood open to rot, mould, mildew.

Sun glare flashed through the window glass. A suggestion of double-exposed imagery floated across the wall.

But when he shifted his head slightly it had gone. Maggie had chosen, and he had to make the best of it. It was her money.

The day after they closed, Wayne had their bedroom ready.

By evening they had the appliances arranged in a rudimentary kitchen. He spent a difficult weekend stocking Maggie's new studio with paints, canvases, and a myriad other supplies.

In her studio he watched as she put the finishing touches on a new painting. Maggie never seemed to mind his visits to her workplace—often she invited him. It didn't seem to matter how unfinished a piece might be.

But then she always acted as if he wasn't there. Her focus could be disturbing, the way she stared at the canvas, aggressively applying paint, not even bothering to check her pigments, holding her breath, unable to do anything else until the canvas filled with colour.

It was one of her house paintings. Almost all of her paintings were of houses, at least as long as he'd known her. Those paintings had proved surprisingly popular in the galleries—they were the reason they could afford to buy this house, and pay for everything else. "They work because the right house will remind us of other houses important in our lives," she explained. "They resonate. You look at certain houses, and you can just imagine the lives of the people inside, trapped by those walls, or lovingly embraced. Their experience is also our own."

When Maggie painted, it was always an attack upon the canvas. She thickened the acrylic paint until it was the consistency of brilliantly coloured liquid clay. She shovelled the colour onto the surface, and then worked quickly to create vegetation, planks, timbers, brick, doors, windows, roofs, sky. He was always surprised when her fury suddenly turned a chaos of swirling thick colour into something recognisable.

But what was even more surprising was that something extraordinarily appealing resulted from this process. These were the prettiest, most intensely welcoming houses he'd ever seen.

"So what do you think?" she asked.

The painting was like all the others, but he could sense subtle differences. "The lines around the door, the porch roof, that window, it's like this house, isn't it?"

"In better days, yes. Or maybe the way it will be, after we finish fixing it up."

"So this place is the model you were looking for?"

"Maybe I've been painting it since the beginning, the spaces, and the lines. It's like I was trying to recall it."

"Then you've been here before?"

"No—I'm sure I haven't."

"Maybe with your dad?" It was a risk—her father had always been a sore point.

"No—I don't think so. The house he moved into after the divorce may have been similar. I stayed there summers until I graduated from high school, a few years before his death."

"It would have helped if I'd known what we were looking for."

"I couldn't have put it into words before now. I'm a picture person, not a word person. I had to see it, be inside it, and then start painting it. That's the way I've always found out things about myself. I've never been here, Wayne, but maybe someone like me lived here or at least nearby. Someone I'm in sympathy with."

"So—living with your dad, that was hard?"

She nodded silently, and then the tears began to drop. He started toward her but she held up her hand. "Sorry. I don't know why I get like this. It was a sad time, but you know how kids are. You can't think of much outside yourself. I'm not aware of hating that house, but I don't remember ever actually being in it. I remember saying goodbye to my mom, and starting out on this long bus trip, but I can't remember ever arriving, living with my dad, or anything about his house. I do remember telling my mother I could never go back, and my mother telling me I had to go back."

He listened, but he couldn't take his eyes off the new canvas. There was an out-of-place shadow peeking out of the upstairs front window: faded, sepia-coloured, uninvited.

Maggie worked late into the evening. Early the next morning Wayne left the house so as not to disturb her sleep. It was cold for working outdoors, but he could at least clear some of the dead vegetation out of the back yard.

He removed a large quantity of dead brush before he could see the ground. And even after he'd got rid of the taller plants he'd get the occasional slap, the random clawing from some unseen branch or stalk, like an untrimmed fingernail tracing the skin. Nothing terribly serious, but enough to well the blood.

A blurred shadow loomed beyond the last sweep of netted branches. With his sleeve he brushed a gritty paste of chaff and blood from his face. "Maggie? You're up?" But when his vision cleared, no one was there. He exhaled in exasperation. The fogged air hung suspended, as if poised.

As he removed dead flowers, the stray remains of potatoes, an onion or two, he began finding ash spread under everything, and bits of foundation from an old wall. An impatient weight crouched nearby, waiting for him to look up, which he eventually did, and found nothing. That was when he heard Maggie yelling from inside the house.

She was on her hands and knees in her studio. He dropped beside her and laid one hand gently on her back. "What happened?"

She shook her head, ran a finger up and down one of the wide gaps between the floor planks. Extensive sections of the ceiling below were missing, so that he could see most of the living room on the first floor.

"I don't know what time I got to bed last night, but when I woke up I was anxious to get back to the painting. Then as I was picking up the brush I smelled something—I don't know—smoky, but terribly sour as well, like overpowering body odour. I felt threatened, as if the stench might smother me. I looked down, and there was this person standing under me. His clothes were dark, dripping, and greasy. And then he shifted, and he was looking at me. Two white, shiny spots staring up at me, but Wayne, no pupils."

It took him minutes to check the house and yard. He rushed in to tell her he'd found nothing. She was still sitting on the floor, shaking. "You say you just woke up. It was probably just a shadow, the light confusing you."

She shook her head. Then Wayne noticed the new painting.

Despite the obscuring strokes of shadow and translucent mist it was still recognisably the same house, but done in a much darker colour palette: greys, burnt umber, deep purple, shades of black and the evening blues. Deepest night. Deepest dream.

"I probably won't be able to sell my usual clients this one."

"Unwelcoming is the word, I guess."

"It terrifies me."

"Then stop working on it."

"I really don't think I can paint anything else until I can finish this one."

It was powerful. A series of vaguely realised trees led you to the front porch, caked in soot, deteriorating under the assault of some oily disease. A gauze of fog hung from the porch roof. But something more: a blurred presence seemed to be arriving out of the darkness from the back of the porch. Wayne wondered if it might not be the figure from the upstairs window in the previous, daylight painting, now come down for the evening, and come out.

"I don't know why we came here."

Wayne grabbed her hand. "It's like you said, houses and people resonate. You're here because of someone who lived here before. You're here because of whatever happened to them."

Every evening Maggie worked on the new painting into the early morning hours. Wayne had never known her to take so long with an individual work—usually she finished them in a couple of days. But she revisited the same areas of canvas again and again, applying additional thin layers of sombre colour, constantly revising lines and shades as she apparently grew closer to her vision.

Each morning when Wayne got up he checked the painting: the blurred figure slightly more resolved, its position slightly shifted on the porch, as if it were pacing. After a few more nights it had left the porch, and was making its way up the sidewalk.

Wayne moved forward on repairs to the house and yard, although concerns over Maggie slowed him. He put a ceiling up in the living room, hoping it might comfort her that she no longer had that god's-eye glimpse into their downstairs. The backyard didn't look so much like a refuse pile anymore. The uncovered foundation proved to extend to all points in the yard—the building it once supported the size of a full house. He also uncovered bits of an old flagstone walk leading back to the alley that ran behind the long row of neighbouring houses.

A night came that Maggie collapsed early, and for once he was the late one up, reading, listening.

At first he thought the breathing he heard might be his own—the book, about secrets and lies and misunderstood identities, had made him tense. But when he put it down and laid his hand on his chest, he realised the rapid panting was more distant—somewhere down the hall and up the stairs. As he made that journey the panting grew louder, and the loudness of it made him think of a dog, the way a dog breathes with his entire body, especially when in pain, heaving and exhaling, unlike people who tend to breathe shallowly from their chests.

The pale little blonde girl lay with her back to him across two steps near the top of the stairs. Her body heaved like an injured dog's. Shadows gathered along her spine: hand-shaped bruises, ending in a crown of yellow curls streaked with dark blood.

Something burned his nostrils—an acrid stench of urine.

But he could find no signs of a spreading stain beneath her.

He wanted to say something, but was afraid. And he dared not touch that tender, panting shape. Suddenly, coughing violently, she faded into deep shadow, and then lit up again with each new intake of breath. What could he do for her? Spying on her in her old distress was some kind of violation, so he slowly crept backwards down the stairs. At the last moment her head jerked up, staring at the door at the top of the stairs.

Her body started to slide toward him as she made ready her escape, but he turned and made his way downstairs and to bed.

"Wayne! Wayne, I want to leave!" He awakened with Maggie's face a collapsed moon hanging over him, her fingers clawing his shoulder. "Now! We have to leave! Please, Wayne."

"Of course." He jerked himself from bed, dragging at his pants. "Just let me get a bag."

"No!" she screamed. Shocked, he stumbled backwards onto the bed. "We have to leave! We have to get into the car! Please!"

"Okay, honey. I'm getting my clothes on right now."

She was unsteady on her feet. They stumbled into the hall. Then she cried, "Wait! Wait right here so I'll know where you are." Then she raced away.

Wayne was just outside her open studio door. In the painting the shadow-wrapped figure was almost to the end of the sidewalk, ready to step out of the canvas. The floppy hat was pulled down over his face. That's his house in the yard. That was his poor child on the stairs. They're why we're here.

"Ready! Let's go, Wayne!" She carried a pillow and blanket under one arm, a butcher knife raised in her other hand. He hurried over, pushed down the arm with the knife. "I need the knife! I have to protect myself!" They started down.

She insisted on sitting in the back seat, the pillow in her lap, the blanket over her, the knife ready in her hand. Wayne didn't ask where they were going, just pulled away from the curb.

He knew immediately that things had changed. Roads and houses, fences and fields, rearranged. When he got half-way down their street it ended in a left-hand turn, with nothing ahead where street used to be but a hayfield studded in bales. He didn't know what else to do but follow the turn.

After a short distance he had to turn again. The road narrowed, the pavement deteriorated. Soon they were on a dirt road, and headed back in the direction of the house. Maggie stared out the window intently.

She must have realised about the same time he did that they were actually in the alley that ran behind their house. But it was dirt now, and the houses faced it. She began rocking the pillow in her lap, making soft soothing sounds. "Did you see the little girl, Wayne? Did you see her? She was just like I used to be. We have to tell someone!"

Before they reached their own house, he realized something large was blocking their view of it. Then he understood the buried foundation had suddenly grown an old dilapidated house.

Maggie started wailing when they saw the hulking dark figure by the edge of the road. Their headlights caught a glimpse of an old see-saw, the pale children teetering there, wide eyes reflecting like cats'.

"Oh, Wayne we have to tell, we have to tell! That poor little girl!"

"We will, honey, we will," he promised, although there was no one left alive to tell.

When the man began lifting his face out from under that floppy brim, Maggie was screaming so loudly Wayne couldn't think. And when they'd finally driven past, and made the next turn that would drag them around that house again, Wayne couldn't imagine how they would ever get off that road.

Wheatfield with Crows

Sometimes when he sketched out what he remembered of that place, new revelations appeared in the shading, or displayed between the layering of a series of lines, or implied in a shape suddenly suggested in some darker spot in the drawing. The back of her head, or some bit of her face, dead or merely sleeping, he could never quite tell. He was no Van Gogh, but Dan's art still told him things about how he felt and what he saw, and he'd always sensed that if he could just find her eyes among those lines or perhaps even in an accidental smear, he might better understand what happened to her.

In this eastern part of the state the air was still, clear and empty. An over abundance of sky spilled out in all directions with nothing to stop it, the wheat fields stirring impatiently below. Driving up from Denver, seeing these fields again from such distance, Dan thought the wheat appeared nothing special. He made himself think of bread, and the golden energy that fed thousands of years of human evolution, but the actual presence of the grain was drab, if overwhelming. When he'd been here as a child, he'd thought these merely fields full of weeds. But so tall, they had been pretty much all he could see, a sea of weeds, wild and uncontrolled. But when he was a child everything was like that—so limitless, so hard to understand.

In the decade and a half since his sister's disappearance, Dan had been back to this tiny no-place by the highway only once, when at fifteen he'd stolen a car to get here. He'd never done anything like that before, and he wasn't sure the trip had accomplished anything. He'd just felt the need to be here, to try and understand why he no longer had a sister. And although the wheat had moved, and shuddered, and acted as if it might lift off the ground to reveal its secrets, it did not, and Dan had returned home.

Certainly this trip—driving the hour from Denver (legally this time), with his mother in the passenger seat staring catatonically out the window—was unlikely to change anything in their lives. She'd barely said two words since he picked her up at her apartment. He had to give her some credit, though—she had a job now and no terrible boyfriends in her life as far as he knew. But it was hard to be generous.

Roggen, Colorado, near Interstate 76 and Colorado Road 73, lay at the heart of the state's grain crop. "Main Street" was a dirt road that ran alongside a railroad track. A few empty store fronts leaned attentively but appeared to have nothing to say. The same abandoned house he remembered puffed out its grey-streaked cheeks as it continued its slow-motion collapse. The derelict Prairie Lodge Motel sat near the middle of the town, its doors wide open, various pieces of worn, overstuffed furniture dragged out for absent observers to sit and watch.

Every few months when Dan did an internet search, it came up as a "ghost town". He wondered how the people who still lived here—and there were a few of them, tucked away on distant farms or hiding in houses behind closed blinds—felt about that.

"There, there's where it happened," his mother whispered, tapping the glass gently as if hesitant to disturb him. "There's where my baby disappeared."

Dan pulled the car over slowly at this ragged edge of town, easing carefully off the dirt road as he watched for ditches, holes, anything that might trap them here longer than necessary. They'd started much later than he'd planned. First his mother had been unsure what to wear, trying on various outfits, worrying over what might be too casual, what might be "too much". Dan wanted to say it wasn't as if they were going to Caroline's funeral, but did not. His mother had put on too much makeup, but when she'd asked how she looked he was reluctant to tell her. The encroaching grief of the day only made her face look worse.

Then she'd decided to make sandwiches in case they got hungry, in case there was no place to stop, and of course out here there wouldn't be. Dan had struggled for patience, knowing that if they started to argue it would never stop. It had been mid-afternoon by the time they left Denver, meaning this visit would have to be a short one, but it just couldn't be helped.

As soon as he stopped the car his mother was out and pacing in front of the rows of wheat that lapped the edge of the road. He got out quickly, not wanting her to get too far ahead of him. The clouds were lower, heavier, leaking darkness toward the ground in long narrow plumes. He could see the wind coming from a distance, the fields farther off beginning to move like water rolling on the ocean, all so restless, aimless, and, by the time the disturbance arrived at the field where they stood, the wind brought the sound with it, a constant and persistent crackle and fuzz, shifting randomly in volume and tone.

It occurred to him there was no one in charge here to watch this field, to witness its presence in the world, to wonder at its peace or fury. No doubt the owners and the field hands lived some distance away. This was the way of things with modern farming, vast acreages irrigated and cultivated by machinery, and nobody watched what might be going on in the fields. It had been much the same when Caroline vanished. It had seemed almost as if the fields had no owners, but were powers unto themselves, somehow managing on their own, like some ancient place.

Dan took continuous visual notes. He itched to rough these into his typical awkward sketches, but although he always kept sketching supplies in the glove compartment he couldn't bring himself to do so in front of his mother. He never showed his stuff to anyone, but his untrained expressions were all he had to quell his sometimes runaway anxiety.

So like Van Gogh's "Wheatfield with Crows", Dan saw long angular shadows carved into the wheat beginning to lift out of their places, turning over then flapping, and rising into the turbulent air where they became knife rips in the fabric of sky.

"She was right here, right here." His mother's voice was like old screen shredding to rust. She was standing near the edge of the field, her head down, eyes intent on the plants as if waiting for something to come out of the rows. "My baby was *right here.*"

The wheat was less than three feet tall, even shorter when whipped back and forth like this, a tortured texture of shiny and dull golds. At six, his sister had been much taller. Had she crouched so that her head didn't show? Had she been brave enough to crawl into the field? Or had she been taken like his mother always thought, and dragged, her abductor's back hunched as he'd pulled her into the rows of vibrating wheat?

Out in the field the wheat opened and closed, swirling, now and then revealing pockets of shade, moments of dark opportunity. The long flexible stalks twisted themselves into sheaves and limbs, humanoid forms and moving rivers of grainy muscle, backs and heads made and unmade in the changing shadows teased open by the wind. Overhead the crows screeched their unpleasant proclamations. Dan could not see them but they sounded tormented, ripped apart.

His mother knelt, wept eerily like a child. He had to convince himself it wasn't Caroline. He stepped up behind his mother and laid his hand on her shoulder, confirming that she was shaking, crying. His mother reached up and laid her hand over his, mistaking his reality check for concern.

A red glow had crept beneath the dark clouds along the horizon, and that, along with the increasingly frayed black plumes clawing the ground, made him think of forest fires. But there were no forests in that direction to burn—just sky, and wheat, and wind blowing away anything too insubstantial to hold on.

Suddenly a brilliant blaze silvered the front surface of wheat and his mother sprang up, her hands raised in alarm. Dan looked around and, seeing that the pole lamp behind them had come on automatically at dusk, he turned her face gently in that direction and pointed. It seemed a strange place for a street lamp, but he supposed even the smallest towns had at least one for safety.

That light might have been on at the time of his sister's disappearance. He'd been only five, but in his memory there had been a light that had washed all their faces in silver, or had it been more of a bluish cast? There had been Caroline, himself, their mother, and Mom's boyfriend at the time. Ted had been his name, and he'd been the reason they were all out there. Ted said he used to work in the wheat fields, and Dan's mother said it had been a long time since she'd seen a wheat field. They'd both been drinking, and impulsively they took Caroline and Dan on that frightening ride out into the middle of nowhere.

Ted had interacted very little with Dan, so all Dan remembered about him was that he had this big black moustache and that he was quite muscular—he walked around without his shirt on most of the time. Little Danny had thought Ted was a cartoon character, and how it was kind of nice that they had a cartoon character living with them, but like most cartoon characters Ted was a little too loud and a little too scary.

"I never should have dated that Ted. We were all pretty happy until Ted came along," his mother muttered beside him now. She hadn't had a drink in several years as far as he knew, but like many long time drinkers she still sounded slightly drunk much of the time—drink appeared to have altered how she moved her mouth.

This was all old stuff, and Dan tuned it out. His mother had always blamed ex-husbands and ex-boyfriends for her mistakes, as if she'd been helpless to choose, to do what needed to be done. Just once Dan wished she would do what needed to be done.

When Dan had come here at age fifteen it had been the middle of the day, so this oh-so-brilliant light had not been on. He hadn't wanted to be here in the dark. He didn't want to be here in the dark now.

But the night his sister Caroline disappeared had also been bathed in this selective brilliance. That high light had been on that night as well. No doubt a different type of bulb back in those days. Sodium perhaps, or an arc light. Dan just remembered being five years old and sitting in the back of that smelly old car with his sister. The adults stank of liquor, and they'd gotten out of the car and gone off somewhere to do something, and they'd told Danny and Caroline to stay there. "Don't get off that seat, kids," his mother had ordered. "Do you hear me? No matter what. It's not *safe*. Who knows what might be out there in that field?"

Danny had cried a little—he couldn't even see over the back of the seat and there were noises outside, buzzes and crackles and the sound of the wind over everything, like an angry giant's breath. Caroline kept saying she needed to go to the bathroom, and she was going to open the car door just a little bit, run out and use the bathroom and come right back. Dan kept telling her no, don't do that, but Caroline was a little bit older and never did anything he said.

The only good thing, really, had been the light. Danny told himself the bright light was there because an angel was watching over them, and as long as an angel was watching nothing too terrible could happen. He decided that no matter how confusing everything was, what he believed about the angel was true.

Caroline had climbed out of the car and gone toward the wheat field to use the bathroom. She'd left the car door part way open and that was scary for Danny, looking out the door and seeing the wheat field moving around like that, so he had used every bit of strength he had to pull the car door shut behind her. But what if she couldn't open the door? What if she couldn't get back in? That was the last time he saw his sister.

"I left you two in the car, Dan. I told you two to stay. Why did she get out?"

Dan stared at his mother as she stood with one foot on the edge of the road, the other not quite touching, but almost, the first few stalks of wheat. Behind her the rows dissolved and reformed, shadows moving frenetically, the spaces inside the spaces in constant transformation. He'd answered her questions hundreds of times over the years, so although he wanted to say *because she had to go to the bathroom, you idiot*, he said nothing. He just watched her feet, waiting for something to happen. Overhead was the deafening sound of crows shredding.

There used to be a telephone mounted below the light pole, he remembered. He and his mother and Ted had waited there all those years ago until a highway patrolman came. Ted and his mother had searched the wheat field for over an hour before they made the call. At least that's what his mother had always told him. Danny had stayed in the car with the doors shut, afraid to move.

He guessed they had looked hard for his sister, he guessed that part was true. But they obviously did a bad job because they never found her. They also told the officer they had been standing just a few feet away at the time, gazing up at the stars. What else had they lied about?

The brilliant high light carved a confusing array of shadows out of the wheat, Dan's car, and his mother. His own shadow, too, was part of the mix, but he had some difficulty identifying it. As his mother paced back and forth in front of the field, her shadow self appeared to multiply, times two, times three, more. As the wind increased the wheat parted in strips like hair, the stalks writhing as if in religious fervour, bowing almost horizontal at times, the wind threatening to tear out the plants completely and expose what lay beneath. Pockets of shadow were sent running, some isolated and left standing by themselves closer to the road. Dan could hear wings flapping over him, the sound descending as if the crows might be seeking shelter on the ground.

"She might still be out there, you know," his mother said. "I was so confused that night; I just don't think we covered enough of the field. We could have done a better job."

"The officers searched most of the night." Dan raised his voice to be heard above the wind. "They had spotlights, and dogs. And volunteers were out here the rest of the week looking, and for some time after. I've read all the newspaper articles, Mom, every single one. And even when they harvested the wheat that year, they did this section *manually*, remember? They didn't want to damage—they wanted to be careful not to—" He was trying to be careful, calm and logical, but he wasn't sure he even believed what he was saying himself.

"They didn't want to damage her *remains*. That's what you were trying to say, right? Well, I've always thought that was a terrible word. She was a sweet little *girl*."

"I'm just trying to say that after the wheat was gone there was nothing here. Caroline wasn't here."

"You don't know for sure."

"What? You think she got ploughed under? That she's down under the furrows somewhere? Mom, it's been *years*. Something would have turned up."

"Then she might be alive. We just have to go find her. I've read about this kind of thing. It happens all the time. They find the child years later. She's too scared to tell all these years, and then she does. There's a reunion. It's awkward and it's hard, but she becomes their daughter again. It happens like that sometimes, Danny."

He noticed how she called him by his childhood name. Danny this and Danny that. It was also the only name Caroline had ever had for him. But more than that, he was taken by her story. To argue with his mother about such a fairytale seemed too cruel, even for her.

He barely noticed the small shadow that had fallen into place not more than a foot or two away from her, a dark hollow shaking with the wind, perhaps thrown out of the body of wheat, vibrating as if barely whole or contained, its edges ragged, discontinuous. At first he thought it was one of the large crows that had finally landed to escape the fierce winds above, ready to take its chances with the winds blowing along the ground, but its feathers so damaged, so torn, Dan couldn't see how it could ever fly again.

Until it opened its indistinct eyes, and looked at him, and he knew himself incapable of understanding exactly what he was seeing. If he were Van Gogh he might take these urgent, multi-directional slashes and whorls and assemble them into the recognisable face of his sister Caroline, whose eyes had now gone cold, and no more sympathetic or understandable than the other mysteries that travelled through the natural and unnatural world.

His mother wept so softly now, but he was close enough to hear her above the wind, the hollowed-out change in her voice as this shadow gathered her in and took her deep into the field.

And because he had no right to object, he knew that this time there would be no phone call, there would be no search.

Acknowledgements

Special thanks to Brian J. Showers
and Melanie Tem for their editorial assistance.

"Here With The Shadows" originally appeared in
Better Weird: A Tribute to David B. Silva,
edited by Paul Olson, Cemetery Dance, 2013.

"A House by the Ocean"
appears here for the first time.

"The Cabinet Child"
originally appeared in *Phantom*,
edited by Paul Tremblay and Sean Wallace,
Prime Books, 2009.

"The Still, Cold Air"
appears here for the first time.

"G is for Ghost"
appears here for the first time.

"Breaking the Rules"
originally appeared in *Narrow Houses*,
edited by Peter Crowther, Little Brown, 1992.

Here with the Shadows

"The Slow Fall of Dust in a Quiet Place"
originally appeared in *Shadows and Silence*,
edited by Barbara and Christopher Roden,
Ash Tree, 2000.

"Inside William James"
originally appeared in *Acquainted With the Night*,
edited by Barbara and Christopher Roden,
Ash Tree, 2004.

"Back Among the Shy Trees"
originally appeared in *Shadows & Tall Trees*, Issue 2,
edited by Michael Kelly, Autumn 2011.

"Seeing the Woods"
originally appeared in *Matter*, Issue 11,
Wolverine Farm Publishing, 2008.

"Smoke in a Bottle"
originally appeared in *Appalachian Winter Hauntings:
Weird Tales from the Mountains*,
edited by Michael Knost and Mark Justice,
Woodland Press, 2009.

"Est Enim Magnum Chaos" originally appeared in
Sorcery and Sanctity: A Homage to Arthur Machen,
edited by Daniel Corrick and Mark Samuels,
Hieroglyphic Press, 2013.

"These Days When All is Silver and Bright"
originally appeared in *Supernatural Tales*, Issue 21,
edited by David Longhorn, Summer 2012.

Acknowledgements

"Telling" originally appeared in
The Seventh Black Book of Horror,
edited by Charles Black,
Mortbury Press, 2010.

"Wheatfield with Crows"
originally appeared in *Dark World: Ghost Stories*,
edited by Timothy Parker Russell,
Tartarus Press, 2013.

"Smuggling the Dead" by Jason Zerrillo originally
appeared as interior artwork in Lawrence C. Connolly's
Voices: Tales of Horror, Fantasist Enterprises, 2011.

About the Author

Steve Rasnic Tem's writing career spans over forty-five years, including more than 500 published short stories, seventeen collections, eight novels, and miscellaneous poetry and plays. His collaborative novella with his late wife Melanie, *The Man On The Ceiling*, won the World Fantasy, Bram Stoker, and International Horror Guild awards in 2001. He has also won the Bram Stoker, International Horror Guild, and British Fantasy Awards for his solo work, including *Blood Kin*, winner of 2014's Bram Stoker for novel. In 2024 he received the Horror Writers Association Lifetime Achievement Award.

SWAN RIVER PRESS

Founded in 2003, Swan River Press is an independent publishing company, based in Dublin, Ireland, dedicated to gothic, supernatural, and fantastic literature. We specialise in limited edition hardbacks, publishing fiction from around the world with an emphasis on Ireland's contributions to the genre.

www.swanriverpress.ie

"While small publishers often produce beautiful books, few can match those from Swan River Press."

– Washington Post

"It [is] often down to small, independent, specialist presses to keep the candle of horror fiction flickering . . . "

– The Irish Times

"Swan River Press—cutting edge of New Gothic."

– Joyce Carol Oates

"The redoubtable Brian J. Showers [keeps] the myriad voices of Irish fantasy alive there in Dublin."

– Alan Moore

YOU'LL KNOW WHEN
YOU GET THERE

Lynda E. Rucker

A woman returns home to revisit an encounter with the numinous; couples take up residence in houses full of sinister secrets; a man fleeing a failed marriage discovers something ancient and unknowable in rural Ireland . . .

In her introduction, Lisa Tuttle observes that "certain places are doomed, dangerous in some inexplicable, metaphysical way", and the characters in these stories all seem drawn in their own ways to just such places, whether trying to return home or endeavouring to get as far from life as possible. These nine stories by Shirley Jackson Award winner Lynda E. Rucker tell tales of those lost and searching, often for something they cannot name, and encountering along the way the uncanny embedded in the everyday world.

"Indirection is a special skill and it's one that Lynda E. Rucker uses frequently to emphasise those near indefinable moments of social alienation and paranoia, that you just want to get up and run far, far away from."

– Adam L. G. Nevill

"Lynda is the genuine article—a serious, literary author of 'quiet horror' whose work is disquieting, inspiring, and oddly reassuring. It's good to know that there are writers so gifted working in our genre."

– *Supernatural Tales*

GHOSTS

R. B. Russell

Ghosts contains R. B. Russell's debut publications, *Putting the Pieces in Place* and *Bloody Baudelaire*. Enigmatic and enticing, they combine a respect for the great tradition of supernatural fiction, with a chilling contemporary European resonance. With original and compelling narratives, Russell's stories offer the reader insights into the more hidden, often puzzling, impulses of human nature, with all its uncertainty and intrigue. There are few conventional shocks or horrors on display, but you are likely to come away with the feeling that there has been a subtle and unsettling shift in your understanding of the way things are. This book is a disquieting journey through twilight regions of love, loss, memory and ghosts. This volume contains "In Hiding", which was shortlisted for the 2010 World Fantasy Awards.

*"Russell's stories are captivating for their
depth of mystery and haunting melancholy."*

– Thomas Ligotti

"Russell deals in possibilities beyond the rational."

– Rue Morgue

*"Quiet horror told in an unassuming,
polished narrative style."*

– Hellnotes

SPARKS FROM THE FIRE

Rosalie Parker

The stories in *Sparks from the Fire* explore a wide variety of familiar characters and settings, yet there is always something else—a shadow world that haunts, disturbs, and threatens. Sons and daughters, mothers and fathers, recluses and lovers—all find themselves shifting between realities: the prosaic and the mystical, even between life and death. The horrors and wonders of these parallel existences are often glimpsed, sometimes revealed, and occasionally overwhelm. These nineteen tales inhabit a terrain in which the uncanny may at any time intrude into everyday life.

> *"[Parker's] treatment of the fantastic is often so light and ambiguous that stories in which it does manifest are of a piece with tales such as 'Jetsam' and 'Job Start', sensitive character sketches whose celebration of life's unforeseen surprises will appeal to fantasy fans as much as the book's more overtly uncanny tales. Parker proves herself a subtle and versatile writer."*

– Publishers Weekly

> *"If you prefer spending dark evenings with a single author, consider . . . Rosalie Parker's* Sparks From the Fire, *which collects nineteen stories, some set against the brooding Yorkshire landscape."*

– Michael Dirda, *Washington Post*